Saving Alessandra

Christine Maria Jahn

To: FAY —

Always a joy to see your sweet smiling face at Church. I hope you enjoy the book.
Love & Blessings!
CMJahn

This is a work of fiction. Names, characters, places, and incidents are products of the author's imagination or are used fictitiously. Any resemblance to actual events, locales, organizations, or persons, living or dead, is entirely coincidental.

Copyright © 2012 Christine Maria Genthner
ISBN: 1449550045
ISBN-13: 978-1449550042

All rights reserved. No part of this book may be used, reproduced, recorded, or transmitted in any manner whatsoever without written permission from the copyright owner.

Printed in the U.S.A.

For my three beautiful daughters: Tabitha, DeAnna, and Julianna. You are the joys of my life and I love you immensely.

And for my dad: it was your love of crossword puzzles that began my love of words. I miss you.

Saving Alessandra

Chapter One

Alessandra Journal Entry, London, 2 April 1816

I saw him today. Him! Simon Thane Bevan, Marquess of Heavensford. The sight of him has awakened so many memories. I was his constant shadow. "Forever in the way!" my dear brother always ranted. But that was so long ago.

I have not seen the marquess during these past eight years, not since I was sixteen.

I relive my departure from England every single day, hoping to wake up from this incessant night terror. Against my screams and tantrums, my industrious father swept me away to America. His decision to leave our estates in the care of my older brother, in order to follow an investment in a shipyard, nearly destroyed my life.

At my father's urging, I married a man who was on the brink of becoming a prominent ship builder. The match seemed logical to my father. And at the time I thought even a bit romantic. But what did I know? I was an innocent, believing in a happily-ever-after.

And my endearing father. He meant well. In my heart I know truly he did. How foolish he was. But more the fool was I.

Just barely out of the schoolroom, I had become

starry-eyed for this man who claimed his love and devotion to me upon our first meeting. It soon became apparent after my father's death, however, that my fairytale marriage was no more.

The suffering I endured at the wicked hands of my outwardly respectable husband was not noticeable at first. Verbal torment he made sure no one could hear. But that soon turned into physical abuse, which became more frequent and harder to keep secret.

I was not allowed to leave my chambers without his thorough inspection to ensure his beloved treatment of me was concealed. Bruises on my neck were hidden with excessive necklaces and lace collars. Bite marks were left in the most discreet places.

One by one he dismissed the entire household staff, except for the butler, who also acted as his valet; one cook, who had the dual role of housekeeper; and one maid, whom he chose for me himself. He blamed his decision on thievery. But I knew different. It was to keep me forever enclosed in his sadistic cocoon.

Thus, with a near empty house, my torture intensified. But none as painfully permanent as my twice broken left hand. A punishment bestowed upon me for taking off my wedding ring. "You should have learned the first time!" my husband yelled. I did not intend to cause his rage. I tried to explain that playing the pianoforte was easier for me with unadorned fingers. "Insubordinate!" he called me, before slamming the fallboard down. I moved my hands quickly, but not quick enough. I was not allowed to cry or I would feel his wrath again.

I had then realized I would never be released from the hell that was my home. And I was forever to be alone. I prayed for God's mercy every night, begging Him to take my life in order to spare me any further agony. I was losing all faith. Until the unexpected, yet glorious, death of my husband.

Chapter Two

Alessandra Journal Entry, London, 3 April 1816

A missive arrived this morning, trudged through the rain by special messenger. I must admit it frightened me for I was not expecting a post.

The writing on the outside of the vellum was not familiar at first. Until I saw the seal. It was from him! The marquess. How did he know I had returned? How did he even see me? I did not seek him out yesterday. Even though my legs were screaming for me to jump from the phaeton and run to him, I could not. I kept my distance.

I broke the seal and opened the missive. The script was perfection compared to my own. I shall never write with such flourish again.

My left hand skimmed over the vellum. The words a blur as tears fell upon my crooked fingers.

Dearest Alessandra,

I thought I was dreaming. Alas! I was not. I saw you from afar and instinctively felt it was you. Then you turned your head and I could see through your black veil, confirming my intuition. Nothing will ever be able to hide your beautiful face. At least not from me.

My condolences on your tragic loss. I was taken aback when I learned of your widowhood. How young you are to be in mourning, only four and twenty. But I apologize. I do not mean to add to your saddened heart.

Would it be too forward of me if I came to see you? Just for a few minutes if that is all you can spare.

My messenger will wait for your reply.
Simon

I was reluctant to answer. I just wanted to be left alone. How I now wish I would have been in an enclosed carriage yesterday, but the weather was too glorious not to relish. The fresh air was most welcoming and I have already spent too many days of my life not being able to breathe without fear.

The poor courier waited with utmost propriety while I pondered a reply. Such a struggle within myself, but I composed a few words. I only pray the marquess will comply with my wishes.

Dear Lord Heavensford,

Please know that seeing you yesterday was a blessing for me. However, it is one I cannot repeat, even from afar. I am not the same girl as when I departed. I need to be alone, confined in peace. I beg you for time, as I am not ready to face the one person who could have saved me.

Regards,
Lady Alessandra Willow Smythson-Drake

The marquess knows my penmanship as if it were his own. But that was when my left hand was able to hold a quill with ease. Now all he will see will be scribbles resembling a student in their first year of classroom learning.

Upon sealing the parchment and handing it to the messenger, he left. I'm sure he was as grateful as I.

Chapter Three

Alessandra Journal Entry, London, 2 May 1816

Roses. He remembered I love roses. The sweet scent of the cabbage rose is a soothing pleasure for my soul as I have been rather tormented these past four weeks. I do not know how I can explain such personal demons to someone who once vowed he was my warrior and protector. My brother doesn't even know of my internal purgatory. Oh, he has seen my disfigurement. I told him it was an accident. I know he suspects it was not, but he has been kind to not ask questions.

So if I cannot talk to my brother, how can I reveal my soul to the marquess? If only my mother had not succumbed to the fever. She would have fought for me. She knew my heart beat for the marquess. But my father gave it to another upon her death. One, who as it turned out, was not deserving of any part of me.

It is strange to be home, yet it is as though I had never left. The furnishings have not change. Nor have any of the servants. Ah, the servants. All dears they are, especially Cook. No questions have been put forth, although I feel their stares. I remain in my chambers for a good part of the day as I hate the stares of pity. I once pitied myself as well;

every moment of every day. But I stopped asking God for an answer because I believe I will never receive one. What good will it do me to continue to beg and plead *why me* as I stare up at the heavens? It will not change the past, it won't change my hideous deformity, and it certainly won't change the recluse I have become.

As for the marquess, I have read his latest letter several times. I do not want to see him. Regardless, I sent a response to appease my brother. It will not be easy to hide my crippled hand from the man I once thought I would marry. Hopefully, he will turn a blind's eye like Sebastian and just let it be. I can only pray he does.

Bevan House, Mayfair, London, 3 May 1816

My Lord Bevan,

I pray this note finds you well. I have received your letter, as well as the beautiful cabbage roses. I was surprised you remembered I am partial to that flower.

My brother sends his regards and has stated that if I do not spare you a few moments of my time, then he will drag me out of this house willy-nilly. You see, I have not been anywhere since arriving back to London, as I believe I would feel out of place among people who were once my peers.

So much has happened in my eight years away. Some of it will shock you; and some of it will even anger you, I'm sure. However, all of it is too painful for me to even think about as being part of my life, let alone speaking of it to others.

Therefore, I must insist that should you accept my offer to come to tea, please do not ask any questions of what you may see. This is my only request and one I need you to abide.

My messenger will await your response.

Lady Alessandra Willow Smythson-Drake

Simon drew his brows together as he read the note a second time, concentrating on the two words that made his nostrils flare with indignation. *Shock* and *anger*. He remained in his seat, staring at the letter until the words became nothing more than a blur. He shifted ever so slightly and picked up his quill, trying not to rush his reply.

My Sweet Alessandra,

Why would you feel you would be out of place? You were the sun and moon if I recall. Many hearts were broken when it was learned that your father dragged you away to America. He did not even give us a chance to say our goodbyes.

I have missed your smiling face whenever I visited your brother. He can be rather dull at times, you know. But I digress. I will be honored to come for tea. I shall call upon you two days hence at precisely two o'clock. And in case you have forgotten, I still remain utterly fond of crumpets.

Simon

He placed his seal on the folded sheet of parchment and instructed the messenger to deliver it post haste. He would have questioned the boy before letting him go, except an inner voice told him to ignore the urge. "I will abide, sweet Alessandra," the marquess barely whispered. "For now, I will abide."

Chapter Four

Bevan House, Mayfair, London, 4 May 1816

"What the devil?" Simon flung an arm across his eyes to block out the sun that began to enter through the windows, but it was not enough to shield the brightness from scorching his vision. With a grunt, he pulled a pillow over his face.

"It's too early to bother me, Oakes! There better be a valid reason for your presence."

The valet ignored the marquess' muffled voice.

"Oakes? The reason for this intrusion, especially since I told you last night not to disturb me this morning. And close the bloody drapes!"

Simon lay in bed, his naked body covered only by a sheet from the waist down. Continued movement from the valet elicited additional bellowing from the marquess, as well as the toss of the pillow.

"Come now, old man. Out with it! Why are you insisting on aggravating me?"

Oakes, employed in the Bevan household before the marquess was born, had been the valet and trusted confidante of his lordship the last fifteen years. In spite of the ensuing bellows, Oakes kept his usual dignified

Saving Alessandra

disposition throughout his master's vociferation.

"I beg your pardon, my lord. The Earl of Ashleigh is here to see you. He said it is quite urgent."

"It better be. This is the first time in weeks in which I have no morning meetings to attend. Heaven forbid I take advantage of having a late slumber."

Simon waved Oakes away when he attempted to lay out clothes for him to wear. "Leave me be. Just go tell the earl I will be down shortly. Since he interrupted my sleep, I'm in no mood to worry about putting on a cravat. The best he's going to get from me at this godforsaken hour is a pair of comfortable trousers and dressing robe."

"I thank you for your kind consideration, old chum. It pleases me that I rank so high as to command such respectful attire."

Both Simon and his valet turned towards the door. Leaning against the frame, arms crossed, was the Earl of Ashleigh, the marquess' long time friend, and Alessandra's brother.

"Good grief! I haven't even yet relieved myself."

"Are you requesting some privacy?"

"Well I don't need an audience, you idiot!"

The earl chuckled, always the one to push his friend to frustration. "Don't let me stop you. Please attend to your morning rituals."

Simon raked a hand through his hair, mumbling incoherent vulgarity, as he walked into his washroom.

"Come Oakes. I think the marquess is awake now." Before leaving from whence he came, the earl felt the need for one last jab. "By the way your lordship, you will be so kind as to shave that scruff off your face, will you? I don't believe it becomes your feminine features."

"Out, Sebastian!"

"Okay, okay, I'm leaving. I'll be in the kitchen bothering Cook for some of her delicious crumpets. She always keeps extra hidden just for me."

"Out!"

The earl left amid more chuckles. And even the ever so dignified Oakes could be heard exhibiting a snort.

As it turned out the marquess did shave. He reasoned that since his chances of returning to bed were quite slim, he might as well make himself somewhat presentable.

He followed the scent of crumpets that were now emanating from his study. Upon reaching the entrance, he realized that it was most unusual for his friend to appear at his home so early in the day. Only one thing or one person could have engaged such action from the Earl of Ashleigh. *Alessandra.*

Simon closed the door and sat at his desk made of deep mahogany. He eyed Sebastian with an arched brow while appeasing his stomach grumblings with a crumpet topped with honey. He sipped, no gulped, his tea. Claiming another crumpet before they disappeared from the plate into the earl's bottomless pit, he ended the silence.

"It's Alessandra, isn't it?"

"I'm glad she took my advice and invited you to tea."

"Apparently you gave her no choice. Not that I mind, but I would rather have a lady invite me of her own accord, not because of a threat."

"Yes, well, she needed a little push to break this self-inflicted seclusion. It has me a nervous wreck, not to mention that the servants are on edge as well."

"Whatever for?"

Sebastian grew solemn, taking his time to gather his thoughts before continuing. But there was no way to placate the situation. "She's hurt."

"I can only imagine. She is a widow after all."

"No, I do not mean emotionally, although that's very apparent. I mean physically. And horribly so."

"What do you mean by horribly so? What happened?"

Sebastian left the oversized leather seat he had occupied and stood with his back towards Simon. Realizing there was no way to stop his emotions from showing, he turned back to face the marquess.

"That blackguard! May he rot in the nether world for all eternity! If he wasn't dead already I'd kill him myself! He did something to her, Simon. I know it was him. Alessandra won't talk about it, but I know it was him."

Simon moved around his desk, placed a hand on his friend's shoulder, and guided him to sit once more in the chair he vacated.

"Tell me. Tell me everything you can. How exactly is Alessandra hurt?"

Sebastian composed himself enough to utter a few words.

"Her hand. Her once graceful and delicate hand is no more. It is severely damaged. So much so that her fingers are permanently maimed."

Simon's emotions encompassed anger to sorrow, sorrow to pity, and then from pity back to undeniable rage. Little did he realize that the abominable roar he heard was his own, until Oakes burst into the study.

"My lord?"

But neither man could respond. Instead, the marquess motioned for Oakes to leave. He did so obediently, yet reluctantly. Once gone, Simon reached behind him to grab the missive he received from Alessandra the day before. He extended his arm towards Sebastian.

"Here. This is the note I received from your sister. I will admit I was shocked by the penmanship, but then decided it was due to emotional turmoil from losing her husband."

Sebastian skimmed his fingertips over the words written. He called to mind how lovely and with ease penmanship once was for Alessandra. The difference was almost too much for the earl to comprehend.

Upon seeing his friend's agony, Simon retrieved the missive and threw it into the fireplace. Lighting a match, he burned it, hoping that with its ashes, the now irreversible deformity to which Alessandra must resign herself, will disintegrate as well.

Chapter Five

The marquess propped himself against the edge of his desk, facing Sebastian; his long legs outstretched and crossed at the ankles.

"At the time I didn't understand what she meant by being shocked and angered. But now it makes sense. More than likely there were other instances. Ones we can't see. And ones your father never saw. She mentioned in her first letter that she couldn't face the one person who could have saved her, meaning me I suppose since I asked to visit her. I was baffled by what she had written, but add that to her second note and we can draw some kind of conclusion."

"I'm sure the sadistic savage played the prince charming role until after Father died. He certainly had me fooled when I visited them shortly after their wedding. It seems Drake had everyone fooled. Alessandra most of all."

"Someone like Drake isn't just physically barbaric."

"I know. And that's what keeps me from sleeping at night. I keep reliving the first time I saw her stepping down out of the carriage. She wouldn't let the coachman guide her. She pulled her arm back and lost her balance, almost falling. I thought it strange to see her hand covered by a muff as she always thought them revolting, but once she was in the library with me and took it off, words can't express what I felt."

Sebastian, never one to drink anything stronger than tea until dinner, asked his friend for some brandy before continuing.

"I know I upset her. She saw me looking upon her as grotesque, when really it was shock at the outward sign of abuse. I tried explaining to her that she is not a hideous creature, but my words did not matter. All she saw was my facial expression, but not my emotion behind it."

Sebastian finished his brandy in two swallows and asked for another. He drank it in one gulp.

"Take it easy, Sebastian. You'll rot your insides drinking like that."

"Then hide the amber liquid because I intend on drinking until I feel numb."

"And how will that help Alessandra?"

"It won't. It's intended to help me."

"How so?"

"Don't you see? I'm her older brother. It's my duty to protect her. And I didn't."

"You can't blame yourself, Sebastian. If you do, then you need to share that blame with your father. And also with me."

"No, not my father. He wasn't the same after Mother passed away. And every minute since Alessandra's been home, I keep asking myself, why didn't I stop Father from taking her to America? I knew she didn't want to go. She begged me to talk him out of it. Do you want to know what I said to her?"

"What?"

"I told her that I had enough responsibility looking after Father's estates. I told her...," Sebastian looked away from Simon, needing to compose himself. "I told her I didn't need the hassle of looking after a giggling schoolgirl whose only importance in life was to get married and have babies."

"How very brotherly of you."

"That's not the worst of it. She wrote a missive to your mother. I saw it lying on the tray for the butler to send out."

"I don't remember the duchess getting any note from Alessandra before she left."

"She didn't. I intercepted it."

"Why?"

"I was curious to see what she had written. At the time I was glad to have opened it."

"What did it say?"

"She wanted your mother to take her in."

"She would have, and very happy to do so."

"I know. But just the thought of having Alessandra lingering about anywhere in England still felt like an obligation to me. An obligation I felt I didn't need. But now I know it was an obligation I just didn't want."

Simon walked over to the window, feeling anger towards his friend of many years. And sympathy as well. He knew only too well what obligations and responsibilities were involved in looking after one's estate, especially when there was more than one. Of course, Simon knew his own situation as marquess was a bit more complex than the earl's, but the underlying accountability was still the same.

Simon turned back around to face Sebastian. "You know I should take you outside and beat you to a pulp."

"Please do. I implore you. But know that whatever punishment you give me will never, and I mean never, erase the hurt I caused my sister. Until the day I die, I will never forgive myself. I should have stood up to Father for her. And I should never have read the letter that was meant for your mother."

"Does Alessandra know you had discarded her letter?"

"No. I'm too cowardly to tell her. Maybe in time I'll explain my actions, but not now. It might make things worse. She barely says two words to me as it is. My blatant betrayal will destroy her."

"Unfortunately, I agree with you. However, I will have

to inform the Duchess." Simon put his hand up towards the earl. "Don't argue with me on this, Sebastian. The duchess needs to know in case Alessandra ever asks my mother why she didn't respond to her letter so long ago. And believe me when I say that you will be a lucky man if the Duchess doesn't call upon you herself for it." Simon raked a hand through his hair, trying to keep himself from hurling expletives at his friend. "I don't even know what to say, Sebastian. Alessandra probably felt like my mother didn't want her around."

"I know, I know. I'm sorry. I...I truly am sorry."

"Don't apologize to me old chap. When the time is right, you need to apologize to Alessandra."

Sebastian nodded in agreement before he downed another glass of brandy.

His anger not subsiding, Simon left his friend alone in the study, allowing Sebastian to drink himself into a drunken stupor.

Chapter Six

Music Room, Smythson House, London, 4 May 1816

Alessandra stared at the pianoforte. Knowing it was the servants' day off and that her brother would be gone for hours as well, she felt at ease roaming the halls of her childhood home.

Her maid offered to stay behind, but Alessandra convinced Josie that she should accept the housekeeper's kind invitation for supper so that her young son, Oliver, could play with the housekeeper's grandchildren. "Besides," Mrs. Piper said, "the more, the merrier." And so off they went.

Once the house was empty, Alessandra began her exploration, which led her to the music room. She was blinded at first by the brightness shining through the windows and terrace doors, which had been left ajar.

Alessandra walked slowly around the pianoforte as she gently brushed the fingertips of her right hand along the top, side, and eventually the fallboard, which covered the keys. She looked at the sheet music lying open as if it was summoning her to play.

Taking a deep breath before sitting on the cushioned seat, she exposed the keys with her good hand. Her left lay settled in her lap. Ever so carefully, a graceful finger touched a single key. One by one, Alessandra pressed the ivory notes, then the ebony. After all the notes were sounded, she started the ritual again.

Immersing herself in the melodic tunes that resonated throughout the music room, she closed her mind to the world around her. *Normal. I'm normal.*

Forgetting the limitation of her encumbrance, Alessandra glanced at the sheet music, lifted both hands to the ivories, and without hesitation, began to play. Only it wasn't beautiful musicality she heard in response, but clanging discord.

She stared at her hands, both still resting on the keys. Her perfect fingers gracefully arched and set to play the next chord, while her disjointed fingers were perversely out of place.

It was a moment before Alessandra sat back from the keys. Overwhelmed with grief for her lifeless hand, she bowed her head and began to cry.

Chapter Seven

Alessandra Journal Entry, London, 5 May 1816

It is strange being home. I have secluded myself to my chambers since the failed attempt at playing the pianoforte. And if only to alleviate the staff of awkwardness, I have even forbid myself from walking throughout the house until evening time after the servants have retired.

Sebastian has been most kind, though I am afraid I have set his nerves on edge. I can see the anguish in his eyes every time he looks at me. His questions go unanswered as I refuse to discuss the details of the life I had while I was married.

There are deep rooted scars, both emotional and physical, that I wish to forget. Oh, I know that will never come to be. I am, after all, a mutilated woman with dark secrets who will forever be searching for one night of peace. One night without pain. And one night without absolute fear.

Tea with Simon today was indeed awkward, to say the least. No words were spoken. They didn't need to be. The marquess felt my pain. I saw it in his eyes. As hard as I tried, I could not keep my hand from his view. His questions were there, yet voiceless, as I had requested.

Alessandra stared at the misshapen words on her journal page. Hoping to relieve some of the exhausting pain, she pulled the quill from between her anfractuous fingers. She kept it in her right hand and dipped the tip into the inkwell. She let the quill touch the paper and delicately moved her hand across the page. Her brief moment of accomplishment died as she looked upon the atrocity of unreadable words. Rage surged through her body as she picked up the inkwell and threw it against her chamber door, accompanied by an excruciating scream. The glass shattered, splashing black ink down the wooden panel.

Before she even moved from her chair, loud footsteps approached her door, followed by the booming voice of her brother.

"Alessandra! Are you alright?" But Sebastian didn't wait for her to respond. He burst through and immediately was met by crunching glass under his boots. "What in blazes happened?"

"Nothing. I dropped my inkwell. Nothing more than that."

"Hmm...an inkwell that dropped itself against the door? Thrown is more like it I say."

"Very well, I threw it. What does it matter? I broke it no matter how it hit the door."

Sebastian put up his hand to keep his sister back. "No, don't touch this. I'll have your maid clean it up."

"She isn't here. I gave her errands to run."

"Then I'll get one of the other servants to do it."

"Sebastian, please! It was my doing. I'll clean it. No sense involving others for my deliberate clumsiness."

Just then another set of resounding footsteps was heard running down the hallway. Alessandra knew at once to whom they belonged. *Simon.*

"Is everything alright?"

"Fine as can be. Just a little mishap between my sister

and her inkwell." Sebastian opened the door wider to allow for Simon to fully enter. "Make yourself useful and help me clean this mess up."

Alessandra quickly pulled her black lace shawl down to cover her affliction. Both Sebastian and Simon pretended as if they didn't notice the action. After the glass was removed and little splatters of ink were wiped off the floor, Sebastian closed the door to survey the damage on the inside panel. An enormous black spot dead center. The men tried to make light of the situation, but their jokes regarding Alessandra's perfect marksmanship only made her withdraw even more.

"Well, my dear sister, you have a choice. I can either leave this stain and you can pretend it's an original painting, or I can get one of the staff to clean it. Plain water just isn't working. The housekeeper is going to have an apoplexy either way."

"Fine. Have one of the servants do it. But have it taken care of when I'm not here."

Simon approached Alessandra. Extending his hand, he took hold of her good one and pulled her to her feet. "Come walk with me in the garden. I think you can use some air."

She looked towards her brother to intervene, but he had already left to fetch a servant.

Simon sensed her reluctance. "Don't be afraid of me, Alessandra. We don't even have to talk. Just take a turn about the garden."

His eyes were sincere, his touch comforting, but Alessandra could think of nothing except that he should have kept his promise from years ago and protected her. Though her late husband was not Satan himself, he was a most frightening monster.

Chapter Eight

Alessandra remained elusive during their walk. As hard as Simon tried to get her to speak, whether about the cabbage roses she loved, which had recently begun to bloom, or talk about Sebastian's recent event of splitting his pants while tripping over his own two feet, Alessandra stayed expressionless.

"You know a man could get a complex if he doesn't receive any type of acknowledgement about his good conversational skills."

Alessandra did not turn to look at Simon when she answered. "You said we didn't have to talk. So I'm acknowledging your suggestion of not having a conversation."

"Ahh. Touché. But it is deemed impolite if one does not reply or respond to another's remarks, is it not?"

"I suppose so."

"Well, since I am doing all the talking, most admirably may I add, and quite happy to do so, I believe I deserve some form of gesture for behaving like an absolute gentleman."

Simon saw a glimmer of hope when Alessandra bowed her head, trying to hide a small smile.

"Aha! I knew there was no way a woman could resist

my charm. I must admit I was worried for a minute. I don't think my ego would have been able to stand the rejection if you didn't at least smile at one thing I said."

Alessandra turned and sat on a nearby bench. Simon followed. When he tried to take hold of her left hand, she quickly moved it.

"Please do not touch it, Simon. Let it be."

"Let me see it, Alessandra. I need to see it."

"Why? You already saw it at tea."

"I want to understand what happened to you. At least let me look at it. I'm your protector. Remember?"

"But even as noble as you are, you couldn't fulfill your promise to me."

"I am sorry for that. Believe me I am. But I'm here to protect you now. To help you overcome whatever keeps you in seclusion every minute of the day. I realize you have only been home a few weeks, but if you can just talk to me, it might help you. Don't shut yourself off from the world, Alessandra. Don't shut yourself off from me."

"It is quite difficult for me. As you can see I am not the same person I once was. My life has been forever changed. I have experienced many..." Alessandra could not continue. She let a tear fall, then bowed her head to cry.

Simon knelt before Alessandra, touching his forehead to hers. "It's alright. Even if that is all you can do, then just cry."

He reached for her hand, the one she kept hidden from all to see. Upon his touch, Alessandra jerked it back. But a second touch from Simon was all that was needed. Once he felt her mangled fingers in his palm, he knew he achieved a small feat.

Simon made no sound of disgust or revulsion. Instead, his caress of each finger was gentle as a tear fell on their joined hands. A tear not belonging to Alessandra, but his own.

Quietly, Simon moved to sit beside her. He touched Alessandra's cheek with the same caress and carefulness that he had bestowed upon her disfigured hand. As another tear fell down his face, a feeling of possession came over him. It scared him to think that he could have feelings for her other than that of a friend. But the longer they sat in silence, the more he knew she was deep in his soul. And with that knowledge was an anger that burned so deep for the torture she fell victim to.

Simon took hold of both her hands. "Look at me, Alessandra." She raised her eyes to his. "I vow to you now, with all my being that you will once again be the carefree girl of long ago. You deserve happiness. You deserve love. You deserve life."

"I beg of you, Simon. Do not pledge yourself to quixotic promises."

"*Trust* me, Alessandra."

"I cannot. I had given all my trust to another man and he betrayed me in the most horrendous way."

"I will not force you to trust me. But I do promise that one day you will."

"You are setting yourself up for failure, Simon. I will never, ever, trust anyone again. Especially a man. Not even you, Simon Thane Bevan, Marquess of Heavensford."

"In time you will, Alessandra. I swear my life upon that promise."

"Then you're a fool."

"You say that now, but your view of me will change."

"You know this to be fact, do you?" Alessandra turned her gaze towards Simon's dark brown eyes. "You seem so sure of yourself. But you don't know what it has been like for me. It's so easy for a man to use those two little words. *Trust me.* With the right charm those two little words become seductive. Manipulative." Alessandra turned away. "Deadly."

Simon leaned into Alessandra's ear and whispered ever so gently, "With the right man they mean happiness. Love. Life."

Alessandra wiped away a tear and rose from the

bench.

Simon stayed behind as he watched her walk back towards the house; towards her room of self-inflicted solitary confinement; and towards the unrelenting demons that haunt her every moment of quietude and every hour of wakefulness.

Chapter Nine

Alessandra Journal Entry, London, 20 June 1816

No words have been written these past six weeks. The onslaught of dampness from the continuous rain and cold has my utterly revolting hand aching more than usual. I have been at the constant mercy of eucalyptus oil, and although the liniment does little to help ease the unbearable discomfort, I continue its use, along with wrapping my hand in a warm bandage.

I have welcomed the inclement weather with open arms each morning. It has made my efforts to shield myself from the world unrequired. The rain has done that for me. And the snow. Imagine that, dearest journal. There has been snow! The veil of white has kept the realm away from my doorstep. I hope it will remain so as the papers have dubbed this weather escapade as the *year without a summer*. My self-seclusion will not be questioned by those belonging to the *ton*, God willing. Unfortunately, it has not deterred the marquess. He sent a messenger with a letter through this horrid cold, but I sent it back. I did not read it.

My dear brother had acquired the services of our family physician, hoping upon hope that the esteemed professional would give knowledge that my hand could be fixed. The good doctor, however, said it was unlikely. Even I knew that.

Poor Sebastian. I let the good doctor explain to him that my hand was never reset after each breakage; that the second incident was worse than the first, and thusly, had caused the irreversible fusion of my bones in their hideous state. The news left my brother despondent.

So with much sorrow, the physician left, leaving behind laudanum for when the pain becomes unbearable. Be that as it may, the poison remains in its bottle on my nightstand, unopened. I have not taken a drop for I refuse to do so. I am uncertain as to which is the lesser of two evils; to be awake with all my violent memories and excruciating pain, or to habituate myself in the addictive use of this opium substance.

And who's to say my night terrors would be no more? I have heard stories that laudanum, while meant to induce requiescence, may not suppress my thoughts and images; but instead make them more vivid, possibly resulting in hallucinations or even a state of euphoric madness.

Am I brave enough to risk an exaggerated state of mind? If so, dearest journal, would I live through one dose of this so called medicinal elixir?

Chapter Ten

Bevan House, Mayfair, London, 22 June 1816

Sebastian waited for the marquess in the library. He poured himself a brandy and drank it in one swallow, realizing that ever since Alessandra had been home, his drinking of brandy had become part of his morning ritual.

He put down his glass and glanced upon the society page that lay on the chair next to the fireplace. He picked it up, and noticed a tiny block of imprint related to his sister.

> *Lady Alessandra Smythson-Drake, who once upon a time had exclusive ties to become a future duchess, has been in seclusion ever since returning home to London. It is rumored that she is horribly disfigured.*
>
> *At first her refusal to accept visitors was respectfully understood due to her state of mourning. However, it now seems that Widow Drake is not mourning her husband's death, but ashamed of her deformity.*
>
> *It was not made clear to this reporter of society news what her exact physical absurdity is, and how it came to be, but it does explain her preference for continuous isolation.*

Sebastian crumpled the paper and tossed it into the waste basket. He poured himself another brandy, but Simon spoke before he had a chance to drink it.

"Careful Sebastian, I just had my liquor restocked. You drank me dry the last time you were here."

"Before you lecture me about my drinking, I think we have another priority that takes precedence, do we not?" Sebastian motioned his head toward the chair that now was vacant of the society paper.

"Ah, so you read the article, did you?"

"Yes, and if Alessandra sees that asinine column herself, she'll become more of a recluse. The old ditties of the *ton* and their daughters are nothing but gossipmongers. They'll be buzzing around my house in droves pretending concern for my sister, when in truth it will be nothing more than to get a depraved glimpse of her altered appearance."

"They *can* be a vicious lot. Most of them anyway. I'm sure there are those who were Alessandra's friends before she left that would be kind."

"I couldn't say. Only two have come around and of course Alessandra had our butler turn them away. I know it will not be easy for her, but I was hoping she would be spared the nonsense. How anyone other than our discreet staff knows about her condition is beyond me. She never goes anywhere. And this dastardly weather has only aided her in her quest to remain inconspicuous."

Simon took a seat in the leather chair opposite the window. "So what do you propose, other than partaking of my expensive brandy, of course? Have you found out anything more about your sister's marriage?"

"Not a thing. She is extremely tight-lipped. Not even our family physician would give me details when he examined Alessandra's hand, except to say that it was broken twice, but he wouldn't say how. The little pixie has sworn him to keep those details from me. She's a total recluse, inside and out. I have yet to take a meal with her.

In fact, she even refuses to allow me to sit with her at tea. At least you were able to have that."

"It is most disturbing, I agree. But you must keep trying."

"What about you? You *are* her friend."

"Yes, and you saw how far that got me. I haven't seen or heard from Alessandra in weeks. A missive I sent her a few days ago came back with my seal intact."

"Try harder."

"Sebastian, what, pray tell, do you wish me to do? If she won't talk to you or have meals with you, what makes you think she would have anything to do with me?"

"Alessandra cannot remain in seclusion."

"I agree. But tread lightly, Sebastian. Your sister is in a delicate state. And also in mourning, though it pains me to say it."

Sebastian stood, his facial expression solemn. His words hissed through clenched teeth. "Alessandra's state of mourning is a mere technicality. And one the dead bas..."

Simon arched a brow at his friend.

"Well, you know what he is, and he doesn't deserve to have someone mourn him." Sebastian finished his brandy and handed the empty glass back to the marquess. "Come to dinner tonight. Seven sharp."

"Wait!" Simon grabbed his friend's arm. "Your sister wants nothing to do with me. She returned my missive without reading it, remember?"

"A slight issue that means nothing. She's pushing you away just as she's trying to push me away. We need to show her that it won't work. That whatever happens, we're not going anywhere."

"Sebastian, I made a promise to your sister that she can trust me. I will not do anything irrational. She needs time and I'm not going to do anything to ruin my chances..." Simon stopped himself but not before he knew he divulged too much.

Sebastian raised a brow. "Your chances? What are you

talking about? Wait!" Straight white teeth displayed his appeasement. "You have a plan, don't you?"

"I want her to learn to trust me. And by the way, she doesn't trust anyone if you haven't noticed, including you. That's why she's become a recluse of her own choosing. And yes, I have a plan, but it needs time and lots of it."

"What exactly are you thinking of doing? Never mind. Tell me tonight. I have an appointment to get to and I only stopped by to invite you to dinner."

"I'll be there, but tell Alessandra. I don't want any surprises forced upon her, Sebastian."

The earl walked away without answering.

"Sebastian, get back here! Earl of Ashleigh, I'm talking to you!"

The earl yelled in response without looking back. "We can talk more tonight. Don't forget. Dinner will be served at seven."

The marquess watched his friend depart. "I hope you know what you're doing, Sebastian."

Chapter Eleven

Smythson House, London

Simon sat in a leather wingback chair, his head back, and eyes closed.

"Does Alessandra know I was invited to dinner?"

"Yes...and no."

"What does that mean?"

"Well, I mentioned to her that it would be nice to have you round for dinner sometime. She said perhaps. I said good. I just didn't tell her it would be tonight."

"You're incorrigible Ashleigh."

"Thank you, Heavensford." Sebastian held his brandy up to Simon in salute.

The two sat in silence for a moment before Simon asked curiously, "What happened to your father's shipyard?"

"My solicitor is looking into the legalities on the portion Alessandra's husband owned."

"Did the beast leave her any financial security?"

"Needless to say she'll be taken quite care of here. My father made sure of it in his will. And I will make sure of it as well. As for Drake, all Alessandra would say is that she never wanted for naught while her husband was alive."

"Do you doubt her?"

"No, her jewelry speaks volumes."

"Hmm...gifts of apologies, no less."

"Indeed."

A knock sounded on the study door. Brooks, the butler entered.

"Excuse me, Lord Ashleigh. Lord Heavensford. Lady Drake has requested a tray be sent to her room."

Both men exchanged glances.

"Did she give a reason for her request?"

"She said she was feeling a bit under the weather, Lord Heavensford."

Sebastian spoke. "Brooks, tell my sister that if she does not feel well enough to sit in the dining hall, then the marquess and I...never mind. Just let her be for now."

"Yes, Lord Ashleigh." The butler left, closing the door behind him.

"Apparently your sister is quite adamant about not seeing me. I thought you said she didn't know I would be here this evening."

"If she knows, either she heard the arrival of your carriage herself, or her maid found out and passed along the information. At least she gave an excuse this time, even if it's just to uphold propriety. Usually I'm left to stare at a vacant chair until enough time has passed that I can determine she won't be down."

"So it's another meal without your sister. I'm sure she'll come around sooner or later."

"No, this is going to stop. And I mean tonight."

"Sebastian, you can't force her. She needs understanding. And more time, which I am prepared to give her, but apparently you are not."

"What she needs is to accept the fact that she's home where she belongs. She's among family. She's among people who won't hurt her."

"So what now?"

"Come on. My sister is not going to ignore me. And

Saving Alessandra

she's not going to ignore you."

"Where are we going?"

"Her chambers, to drag her down to dinner."

Simon didn't budge. "Thank you, but I pass. I feel bad enough barging in for dinner, even though you extended the invitation. If you want to drag her down then that's your choice. Not mine."

"Very well. Stay here and be a coward."

"I'd rather be a coward than add to your sister's inner turmoil."

Sebastian departed, doubting his decision the moment he left his study.

Alessandra scolded the men for not abiding by her request to dine alone. She swore under her breath on the way to the dining hall that if her eyes could shoot daggers they both would be bleeding to death at that very moment.

After everyone was seated, an attempt was made at conversation; a few words regarding the weather and new book additions to the library, but nothing more substantial or in great detail.

When dinner was served, a heavy silence befell the room. Sebastian and Simon quickly took to their meals, while Alessandra sat, staring at her plate.

She fumbled the fork when first placed between the second and third fingers of her left hand. Once she felt it was secure, she picked up the knife and tried to slice into the piece of roasted chicken. Success was not to be had.

Alessandra peered up at her brother and Simon; both remained engrossed in satisfying their hunger. She secured her fork once more and decided to cut into a seasoned boiled potato. Once again, no success. The vegetable had a mind of its own, playing a game of catch me if you can with Alessandra's silver, until it rolled off the plate and onto the table.

Frustrated, Alessandra removed the fork from her left hand and dropped it with the knife onto her plate. The fork bounced off, hitting her water goblet, knocking it over.

Sebastian and Simon turned their heads at the noise.

"Are you both happy now? This is why I refuse to take meals with you Sebastian. And why I refuse to invite you to tea again." She looked at Simon before turning her attention back to Sebastian. "It is why I want to be left alone. But you won't let me. I asked both of you to leave me be. But you will not take no for an answer. I cannot exhibit proper social graces or proper etiquette. I am a cripple! Do you not understand that?"

"Alessandra..."

"No, Sebastian. Do not say a word." Alessandra looked at each man, her vision becoming cloudy. "And do not feel sorry for me. I do not want nor need your sympathy. Just leave me be. I am *begging* you to leave me be. *Please.*"

"I'm sorry, Alessandra." Simon softened his voice. "I did not mean for my presence to add such a heavy burden to the one you're already carrying."

"You asked me to trust you, Simon. How can I when even the simplest request gets ignored?"

"Dearest, don't blame Simon. It was my idea. I invited him to dinner. He made it very clear that I must tell you, but I did not."

Alessandra gave a slight snicker. "You're worse than Simon. I can't trust you at all. You want so badly for me to take meals with you, to talk to you. Where was this concern I so desperately needed when I begged you to speak with Father about taking me to America?" Alessandra continued as her brother remained silent. "You don't think I know about my letter to the duchess? I saw you take it. I was even going to confront you about it that night, but thought it was no use. Why should I stay when my own brother wanted me gone? And now, after all these years, you feel obligated to uphold your brotherly duties. Why, Sebastian? Is it because you feel guilty about what I have gone through these past eight years? The hell I have lived every moment of every day? Spare me your sympathy, dear brother, for I have no use for it."

"I want you to believe me, Alessandra, when I say I am truly sorry for what I did. I know I will never be able to make it up to you. I can't even live with myself right now. I can't sleep without getting drunk and I can't get through the day without starting it off with some brandy. If I could go back in time and do it all over again, I would beg Father to let you stay with me. But since that is not possible, all I can do is apologize and pray that one day you will forgive me."

"Forgive you? Are you mad? You ruined my life." Alessandra stood up, looking at each man. "I am begging you both for the last time. *Leave. Me. Alone.*"

Sebastian cleared his throat, his voice held an undeniable quiver. "Of course, whatever you wish."

Alessandra's gaze passed from her brother to the marquess. He, too, gave a slight nod.

For the very first time, Alessandra felt the need to take laudanum.

Chapter Twelve

The air was stifling. Alessandra tossed and turned, tangling herself in the sheets soaked from sweat. Her breathing shallow, she clawed at her face. "Off. Get it off!" Her desperate cries went unheard.

The night terror took control of her every movement. Still grappling with the sheets, she made another attempt to free the imaginary cloth from her face. Red scratches began to appear as her efforts became more violent.

Her whimpers were silenced as she rolled onto her stomach, face down into her pillow. Drops of blood stained the fabric, exposing welts from the scratches.

Her body turned again, but this time by a force that was not her own. Kicking her legs in order to get free, she felt the strength grab hold of her shoulders.

"No, let me go. No more, Cecil. Please no more!"

The hold on her body was strong. Alessandra struggled fiercely to break free, but the force that encompassed her became more powerful. She screamed as it pulled her up to a sitting position.

"Alessandra!"

Sebastian? No, it can't be. Sebastian's in England.

"Alessandra, wake up! Dearest, wake up and look at me!"

With another shake her writhing body ceased its movement. Eyes wide, she saw her brother staring back. "Oh my God! I thought...I mean I was..." Alessandra wrapped her arms around Sebastian's neck. His shirt absorbing her tears.

"Hush, my dearest. It's alright." Sebastian held tight, afraid to let go. "It was only a bad dream," he whispered in her ear as he spotted the opened bottle of laudanum on the bedside table.

Sebastian awoke some time later, muscles aching from sleeping in the corner tufted chair. He stretched his legs, then his arms, before standing. The sun's early rays barely peeked through the lace fabric panels that decorated the window. He opened the sash, filling the room with the scent of morning dew.

His eyes went to Alessandra who lay abeyant. He looked about the room, senses on alert as he pondered if the laudanum could have triggered his sister's nightmare. *No, there's more. Much more. What all did that fiend do to you, Alessandra?*

Sebastian walked towards the bed, picking up the quilt he suspected his sister kicked onto the floor during the night. Raising it to cover her body, he noticed the deep scratches on her face, and dried blood on her pillow.

He clutched the knob on her chamber door, then turned to look at her once more before leaving. "Sleep well today, fragile one. Sleep well."

Chapter Thirteen

Somersby, Ducal Country Estate, Oxfordshire, 26 June 1816

Simon paced back and forth as he recanted to his parents the atrocity that had befallen Alessandra at the hands of her now dead husband. His voice, usually deep and resonant, was now barely audible and broken.

He knelt before his mother, taking hold of her delicate hands. "Mother, such a simple gesture as this, is one of disgust for Alessandra. She is a recluse within her own chambers. She refuses to even take tea with her brother, let alone meals. And now I'm afraid we may have made matters worse."

The duchess sat solemn on the settee of emerald green, the duke stood to her side. They listened with naught a word of interruption, allowing Simon to continue his discourse.

"We ordered her to dine with us. Actually Sebastian did the ordering. I told him to let her be, but he dragged her out of her chambers anyway. Oh, I'm sure he meant well. But in our haste to see her socialize, we nearly destroyed what little dignity she had left of herself. How can we make amends for what we've done?

"If you only saw her face, Mother. We lost her that day. What little hope we had of helping her is gone. I doubt she will speak at all to me when I return to London. I fear we may never know what transpired during her residence in Savannah. And I know her dead husband is to blame for more than just her hand. Someone who is cruel physically is surely to be cruel verbally. And emotionally. But she will not talk about it, only to the physician who reviewed her condition. And sweet Alessandra has sworn the doctor to secrecy. He will not confess what he has learned. And now that article in the paper. She does not need to be cast in the public eye as some hideous creature."

Simon bowed his head from the guilt that consumed him. "I'm sorry Mother. Father. I do not mean to show weakness. But all I thought about the past few days is why didn't her father wait one more day before taking her to America? I missed her departure by just one…single…day. Worse still, why did I not travel with Sebastian when he visited Alessandra shortly after she was married? If only I could go back…save her…steal her away."

"Dearest, you did not know. Neither did your father. Nor I. Her letters were scarce. Never a word mentioned of unhappiness, let alone abuse of the magnitude to which she has encountered. And then her letters stopped."

Simon looked up at his mother. "Sebastian didn't even know. He believes her torture began after their father's death."

"Probably so." The Duke of Somersby patted his son's shoulder. "Come now my son. We will do what we can for Alessandra. However, it seems it will be a long road for this once innocent child to accept her fate as a crippled woman."

"Father! Please do not call her crippled."

"But she is, Simon. She cannot go back to being who she was. You must know that yourself. Apparently she has lived with nothing but evil the past few years. It will take time, but with our love and help, I'm sure she will one day be happy. At least happy enough to accept her life for what it is."

"Simon", the Duchess began, "you have grown into a fine young man. We are very proud of you. We know this tragedy that has become Alessandra's life troubles you deeply. It troubles us as well. Had we any inkling that the poor girl was suffering, we would have taken swift action. But since dwelling on the past will not change it, we need to ask ourselves, what can we do to make her present and her future better?"

"You don't understand. It could have been prevented. She told her father to leave her behind with Sebastian. When he refused, Alessandra begged her brother to talk their father out of it. But Sebastian wouldn't. Then she wrote a note."

"What note?"

"She wrote a note to you, Mother. Asking for you to take her in."

"I never received a note with that request."

"I know. I had only just been told of the note myself by Sebastian. He intercepted it."

"I see. It seems there is a lot of guilt then. For all parties involved."

"Too much for Sebastian to withstand," Simon said. "He's taken to drinking brandy. Quite often, I'm afraid; and to the point that he cannot sleep or get through the day without it."

"Poor Sebastian." The duchess looked at her husband. "We need to help in whatever way we can."

"I agree with you, my love." The duke shifted his attention to Simon. "What would you like us to do?"

"I would like for you to invite Alessandra to stay here at Somersby. At least for a while. She needs to be away from London and prying eyes, but she needs to also be away from Sebastian. She is abundantly angry at him and he drinks away his sorrows, or tries to, because he can't handle seeing his sister in a sullen state. And...I would like to stay here as well. I want to help Alessandra. I *need* to help her. She has no faith in anyone and I promised her that she will trust me one day. That I *will* make her happy."

The duchess cupped Simon's cheek. Her dark eyes stared into his. "It won't be as easy a task as it sounds."

"I know. But I must try. I care for her. Deeply."

The duchess gave a slight smile. "She may never want to be happy, Simon. Or even love you back. Are you willing to take that chance?"

"More than I can express to you in words."

"What was it that you always used to call yourself? Let me think. Ah, yes. Warrior of Heavensford, was it not?"

"And protector of all who live within it."

"She needs to give you her heart first before you can protect it."

"I know Mother. I know."

"Do not venture on this quest, Simon, if you do not wish to have Alessandra as your wife," the duke stated. "For if you play with her heart, and say the things you believe she would like to hear just so your own heart and mind feel at peace, you will forever shatter that girl."

"She is in my soul, your grace. She always was. I just never realized how much until I saw her again."

"Be careful, my son. Do not become misguided in your feelings. Concern and sympathy are sometimes mistaken for love." The duchess added with concern, "If you do this, if you are absolutely certain that you want to help Alessandra, and are sure of the fact that you are in love with her, then do not give up on her. But remember, love doesn't always change people. *She* will need to change herself from the recluse she has become. Offer her guidance, support, friendship. Do not rush her. It may take a long time before she is accepting of your feelings for her. And she may never fully trust you. It is a possibility that she may not want to break free of her solitary confinement."

"I must help her, Mother. I cannot sit idly by and watch her give up on life."

"Then I will pen an invitation to Alessandra post haste. Should I send it by special messenger or would you like to deliver it yourself?"

"I will take it to her. It will give me an excuse to not only check on her, but also Sebastian. I haven't seen either one of them since the dinner fiasco." *And God help that fool brother of hers if I find he's made matters worse.*

Chapter Fourteen

Heavensford, Marquess Country Estate, Berkshire

After Simon was satisfied that all important matters had been discussed and arranged with his parents, he left for his own estate of Heavensford later that day. In his pocket were two missives. The first was a ducal order signed by his father, the Duke of Somersby, to *The Gazette,* requesting a temporary cease from printing further articles that alluded to any deformity pertaining to Alessandra. Simon knew the gossip could not be halted forever, but at least until such time when Alessandra herself would be better able to handle any discussion of her disfigurement. The second was a note to Alessandra from his mother. He hoped that any plans they were about to put into action would result favorably for the girl he once knew, and the woman he both needed and wanted to understand.

The marquess now sat at his small writing desk in his chambers at Heavensford. The box of mementos from long ago was opened, revealing tiny treasures of his youth. Among those he held most dear was a lock of Alessandra's hair, given to him before he left on his one-year journey with his cousin, the Duke of Veston. Simon inhaled the scent of jasmine that still lingered on the curl. *Remember me* he recalled her saying. "Had I only known that I truly loved you then, things would be so different now." Simon put the curl back in the piece of folded parchment, but not until he inhaled the scent once again.

Upon further observance of the cherished keepsakes was a small piece of fabric embroidered with delicate flowers surrounding a sword; the initials *AWS* on one side of the blade and *STB* on the other. A calling card wrapped in the fabric fell onto the desk when the marquess unfolded the square. Seeing Alessandra's printed name in beautifully scripted gold lettering, Simon flipped the card over.

My dearest protector of Heavensford,
Thank you for the lovely silver thimble. You are, and always will be, my warrior.
Love in my heart for you till the end of time,
Alessandra

Simon rewrapped the card in the embroidered fabric, also scented with jasmine oil, and placed it inside the folded parchment with the lock of Alessandra's hair.

The marquess stood, closing the cherry wood box with all his childhood mementos hidden inside, except the jasmine scented parchment containing the gifts from Alessandra. "You will be happy again, sweet one. I promise with every breath I take. You *will* be happy."

Chapter Fifteen

Smythson House, London, 30 June 1816

Alessandra sat on the wrought iron bench in the corner of the garden. It had become her favorite sanctuary when weather permitted it. Her left hand was shrouded by a fur-lined muff, her right hand delicately holding the rose that her brother had placed on her tea tray.

She had resigned herself to the fact that as hard as she tried to avoid being seen or limit any interaction, her determination was futile. She remained adamant in regards to dining alone and turning away visitors, which had been several the past few days.

She had confessed to Sebastian that she had overheard his heated demand to the butler and housekeeper, in which all society papers are forever banned from entering the house. She pressed her good hand to his cheek to stop his forthcoming retort, tenderly stating she understood his reasoning for implementing the request. However, she went on to say, that in doing so, he heightened her curiosity, thus sending her maid scavenging for a copy that had beset his temper a flare in the first place.

Since then, she had forced herself to alleviate some of

her self-inflicted seclusion. Her turns about the house now included the library, the music room, even if only to stare at the pianoforte, and her new sanctuary, the garden.

Admiring the rose still in her hand, Alessandra became aware of another presence. She looked up. *Simon.*

He stood regal, a package in hand.

Noticing his apprehension to approach her, Alessandra dipped her head ever so slightly. She glanced at the milliner's box and wondered what surprise it held. She shifted her gaze back to Simon and was met with a smile.

Watching the marquess increase his pace, Alessandra remembered the little surprises he used to give her years before. One she favored in particular was a gift for her sixteenth birthday; a silver thimble engraved, *from your warrior.* The thimble, although no longer used, remains in her little mahogany box of very few cherished possessions. No one knew about the thimble or the secret message Simon had scripted inside of it. Not even her husband when he was alive. For if he did, Alessandra knew it would have been destroyed.

Upon Simon's nearness to her, Alessandra saw that the box wasn't just from any milliner, but the most prestigious on Bond Street.

Covered with elegant wrappings and luxurious bow, Simon held it out to her.

"For you, Alessandra."

She skimmed her good hand along the side of the box. Her left hand, remained in the muff.

"It's a very pretty box."

Seeing her reluctance to take hold of it, Simon began to unravel the bow.

"No, don't. Let me."

"Of course." Simon placed the box on the bench next to Alessandra.

Her right hand lingered before removing the garment from her left. Her overly warm fingers took delight in the playfulness of the breeze. She pulled the rest of the bow apart and found the lid was not too tight. She removed it and looked inside. .

"Oh my, how exquisite, Simon!"

Sheer gossamer of pale lavender lined with silk of a darker purple had been constructed into a lightweight hand covering, similar to a muff, yet was of a smaller design, just enough to cover her mutilated fingers.

"Do you like it, Alessandra?"

"Yes. Yes I do. Very much. It's beautiful, Simon."

"I hope you don't mind. I know you are in mourning, but I felt a much happier color was needed. Do you find it agreeable? It's your favorite shade of purple if I remember correctly."

"I don't mind. And yes, you did remember correctly. Thank you."

"You're very welcome."

Simon remained standing, watching Alessandra smile. The first smile he'd seen since the last time they were in the garden.

Another breeze blew, enticing the air with Simon's cologne, a mix of sandalwood and musk. Suddenly realizing that he was still standing, Alessandra slid the box over to make room on the bench.

"Forgive me. Please sit down."

"Thank you. I can only stay a few minutes as I have a meeting to attend."

Alessandra struggled with her thoughts. "I...I just..." She looked at the marquess. Dark eyes met her gaze. Speechless, she instead watched Simon move closer, almost touching the edge of her black muslin gown. She inched away, nearly to the edge of the bench. Once again, the marquess' presence took hold of her speech.

"Um...thank you for the muff."

"You have already thanked me, but you're quite welcome...again."

Alessandra bent her head to look at her gift, or so she hoped that's what Simon thought. In truth, she did it mostly to conceal her expression as she didn't know whether to keep smiling as a result of Simon's thoughtfulness, or cry because of the reason for it.

She heard a rustling and turned to face the marquess.

"This is from my mother."

"The duchess?"

Simon nodded.

"She knows I'm back in England?"

"She has only recently become privy to that fact."

"No doubt from *The Gazette*."

"As a matter of fact, no. 'Twas my own doing that informed her."

"Ah, so this is a letter of pity then."

"Alessandra, you know my mother better than that. She cared for you as a daughter when your own mother passed away."

"I know. Forgive me. It was rude of me to preclude her feelings before reading the letter."

"There's no need to apologize." Simon lightly took hold of her chin, tilting her face up towards his own. "Ever."

He leaned in closer. Alessandra felt his breath mingle with her own. Unease suddenly enveloped her. She quickly turned her head.

The marquess cleared his throat. "I will leave you so you can read your missive in private." Simon stood, bowed, then left, leaving behind Alessandra in a state of utter befuddlement.

Sebastian stood by the window in his sitting room, watching the exchange between his sister and best friend. *Did she just smile? Lord, she did! Wait, why are you touching her face, Heavensford? You're leaning in a little too closely, my friend. Back away! Let the poor girl have some air. Ah, good chap. You decided to walk away.*

Sebastian stayed still, continuing to watch his sister. From far away she was flawless. He didn't see any imperfection with her hand. *But what happened to her smile. It is gone. Why?* "Hmm, it seems I need to have a chat with the marquess."

"About what?"

Sebastian jumped. "Bloody blazes, Heavensford, don't sneak up on people like that!"

"Frighten much, Lord Ashleigh?" Simon smirked as he backed away from Sebastian.

"You're lucky I didn't have my sword nearby, or worse, my pistol. You would be lying in your own blood right now."

"For what? Giving your sister a moment of happiness? You should be thanking me, not proposing ways to do me in. And what did you want to chat about anyway?"

"What did you say to Alessandra?"

"Come now, a gentleman doesn't kiss and tell."

"It looked like you *wanted* to kiss her. You were sitting a bit too close to her, were you not?"

"For heaven's sake, Sebastian! Do you hear yourself? I gave her a gift and a note from the duchess. Nothing untoward happened or was going to happen."

"Really? Then why did my sister look like her feelings were hurt when you walked away?"

"What are you babbling about?"

"You mean you weren't going to kiss her?"

"No! And even if I wanted to, I wouldn't tell you about it. And why on earth were you spying on us anyway? Or should I say on me?"

"I wasn't spying."

Simon arched a brow.

"Okay, I *was* spying. But not on you. On Alessandra."

"Why?"

Sebastian leaned against the window and motioned for Simon to take a seat.

"Alessandra's been having terrible dreams. She never wakes up from them until I shake her awake. I'd swear it's like she was living in them at that moment."

"When did these start?"

"The night we had that disastrous dinner. She's had so many of them now. The first one resulted in scratches on her face. The second and third were pretty bad as well. And they keep getting worse. But the last one..." Sebastian shook his head. "She was wide awake. Running to God knows where or why, but she tripped and fell, and ended up with a sore ankle."

"Does she say anything during these episodes?"

"Mainly she just keeps repeating the dead blackguard's name. Keeps telling him she's sorry and that she didn't mean to make him angry."

"The cur lives on then."

"My thought exactly. I've been sitting with her until she falls asleep. But I don't leave once she does. I'm afraid to. I've taken to sleeping in the chair she has in her room. Sometimes I sleep on the floor."

"I think I have some good news for you then. The duchess wants Alessandra to visit with her for a spell."

"I don't know, Simon. She needs to be looked after."

"Don't worry. She'll be with my parents."

"Does Alessandra know about going to Somersby?"

"She will once she reads the missive from the duchess."

"God willing, I hope she's able to get some sort of peace, Heavensford. I don't know what will happen to her if her night terrors get any worse. What if she has another incident during the day time?"

"Maybe she needs laudanum."

"She has a bottle of it. Sometimes it works, sometimes it doesn't. I'm afraid, Simon. I don't know how to help her."

"I'll send a message to my mother to have the duke's physician talk with Alessandra. Maybe he can suggest a better solution from the apothecary. Perhaps something that will ease the pain in her hand as well."

"Please take care of her. Don't give up on her, Simon."

"Put your fears to rest, my friend. She will be taken care of. I promise."

Chapter Sixteen

Alessandra watched Simon leave the garden. Once he was out of her view, she turned her attention to the missive from his mother, the Duchess of Somersby.

She broke the ducal seal, unfolded the parchment, and began to read.

Dearest Alessandra,

I would have written much sooner, but I have only just found out about your return to England. Simon has mentioned your reluctance for any social interaction. While I understand your state of grieving, you are much too young to sit behind closed doors in solitude. Therefore, you must come to visit me at Somersby. I insist.

Love to you always,
Your Second Mama, Duchess of Somersby
P.S. Do not be angry with Simon for telling me.

Alessandra read over the missive once more before returning inside to pen a response. After several attempts, she cried at the horrid sight of unrecognizable words. She resigned herself to employing the help of her brother, but only after Simon's departure from their home; and was exceedingly stubborn to make sure Sebastian wrote her exact words.

Dearest Duchess,

I am truly sorry for not writing to you myself upon my arrival from Savannah, but I am not too fond of the task these days. As you have stated, I am not comfortable with afternoon teas or gathering for dinner with Sebastian and his friends. Or even my peers from long ago. I do not even feel at ease in the presence of your son, which is hard to believe considering I was his most devoted shadow during my schoolroom days.

I know if I do not accept your invitation, I risk insulting your kindness. And that I would never do. I would be most grateful, and honored, to spend some time at Somersby. It would be lovely to see you and the duke again. I will depart within the next few days.

Love to you and the duke,
Alessandra
P.S. I know Simon means well.

Once a servant had been summoned and departed with the letter, Alessandra informed her maid of the impending travel. She then sat in the oversized leather chair that once belonged to her father, and called for tea.

Sebastian looked up in surprise.

"Why do you look at me as if you've never heard me request a tea tray?"

"I'm at a loss for words since you have been most adamant in your endeavors to take tea alone in your room. To what do I owe this extraordinary honor?"

Alessandra gestured for Sebastian to take the seat opposite her.

"I know it was a shock for you when I first arrived home. It has been difficult for you to see me less than normal. It has been most difficult for me, and still is; and probably will be until I die an old widow."

"Don't say..."

"Let me finish, Sebastian, before I lose control of my emotions and start crying like a blithering ninny."

Her brother sat back, allowing Alessandra to continue the speech she practiced in her room for an hour.

"I know you see me as someone less than whole. And maybe I am. In fact, we both know I am. There are many things I can no longer do that were once tasks of such ease. I was too young at the time to realize what I've taken for granted. Do you know I cannot even tie a ribbon? Let alone safely pour a pot of tea? Or butter a slice of bread? Or heaven forbid, cut the food on my dinner plate? Unfortunately, and to my disdain, both you and Simon have witnessed that disaster first hand. Ever since that day, Cook, God bless her, prepares my food so I do not have to worry about it. It is most..." Alessandra lowered her head, "disheartening. I can't even do the most basic function of feeding myself unless someone else cuts my food into bite size pieces. I am not a child, yet I have to resign myself to live like one."

Sebastian leaned forward, taking hold of his sister's hands. To his astonishment, she did not pull back as she had done on previous occasions.

"Listen to me, Alessandra. You are strong and intelligent and most resilient. You *will* overcome these obstacles. Believe that, dearest."

"No, Sebastian. I cannot. There are too many of them. I couldn't even write a note to the duchess. I required your services to do it for me."

"You've written missives before. Your hand was bothering you more today than others. That is all."

"You are very naïve, indeed, Sebastian. I will not just wake up one day and have my hand be normal. I am still trying to fully accept who I am. And how I got this way."

"I know you have suffered greatly. And not just your hand. Please tell me, Alessandra. I wish you would truly talk to me. What all did that devil do to you?"

"I cannot." Alessandra tried to stand, but Sebastian would not let go of her hands. "Please Sebastian. I want to go back to my room."

"No. You need to tell me. I hear your cries at night. I shake you awake from your terrors. I hold you until you are once again reprieved. Now tell me what has happened!"

Alessandra pulled her hands away. She looked up at her brother.

"He killed me, Sebastian. The woman I longed to be...tried to be. A wife. A mother."

"A mother? What..."

"That is the worst of my demons. One that will forever haunt me. And one I will not...no...one I *cannot* talk about. For that malignant spirit is my own personal Hades."

Alessandra rose to her feet, wiped the wetness that fell upon her cheeks, and left.

Sebastian leaned forward, elbows propped on his knees, lowered his head into his hands, and cried.

Chapter Seventeen

Somersby, Ducal Country Estate, Oxfordshire, 5 July 1816

The carriage eased its motion onto the private drive that led from the main road to the ducal residence. Rousing from her sleep, Alessandra pushed aside the window tapestry to scan the front grounds. The sun, on the brink of setting, cast an orange glow through the trees that lined the road on both sides.

Near the end of the path, the house burst into view. Alessandra dropped the edge of the tapestry and reached across the seat to grab her lavender muff. It was not as warm as the other one she had been wearing during the trip, but a sense of obligation to wear the lightweight fabric out of respect for the one who gave it to her enlightened her suddenly.

Feeling a curl come loose from her chignon, she tried to fix it, but couldn't find the hairpin that had fallen, nor was she able to re-tie the ribbons on her bonnet. She pushed the curl behind her ear, but it sprang free. Accepting defeat, Alessandra let it hang loose.

She felt the carriage stop and quickly covered her left hand with the lavender muff as she heard servants and stable hands swift with their movements. The carriage door sprung open and steps pulled down. A large mass was standing to the side. Alessandra did not take notice to whom it belonged. A deep voice greeted her when she grasped an arm for balance.

"Welcome back to Somersby, Alessandra."

She turned her head. "Simon!"

"I trust your journey was uneventful?"

"Quite uneventful, actually."

"Pity. It's been a long time since I used my sword. I was hoping to avenge you by dueling a dandy highwayman or some such. You do remember that I *am* the warrior of Somersby and Heavensford, *and* protector of all women who reside within?"

"Yes, I remember. But I am only a guest. I do not live here."

"The warrior in me sees no difference." Simon looked down at her and winked. Her face held no expression as she stared back. "Is something amiss, Alessandra? You are well, I hope?"

"Yes."

"Good." Simon covered her hand with his own, ensuring she would not escape his presence.

They started up the steps, but Alessandra abruptly stopped. "Simon, wait." She looked up. He towered over her. Realizing she was staring at his chest, she walked up two steps to alleviate the awkwardness of his height. And the shortness of hers.

"The duchess told me this was your suggestion. This visit for the remaining summer."

"Alessandra..."

"No, it's quite alright. I know you are worried for me. As is Sebastian. This...this will be a good place for me."

"If you want to talk...need to talk...I am here for you. Always remember that, Alessandra, will you?"

"I will." She took hold of Simon's arm once again, and together, they ascended the steps.

After being acknowledged with greetings from the line of servants, Alessandra entered the sitting room, nervous to see the duchess after eight years. Simon gave her right hand a slight squeeze before he let go. The duchess instantly took her into a motherly embrace.

"Here, dearest. Let us sit down, shall we? You must be weary from the journey."

Alessandra followed the duchess to the settee that was covered in pale blue fabric.

"That's better. Simon, be a dear and tell Jasper to bring us tea. Then you may leave us."

"Leave you? I take it I am being thrown out?"

"Alessandra and I have much to discuss. And it will be for my ears only."

Both Simon and Alessandra knew there was nothing either one could say. Questions put forth by the duchess would not go unanswered.

"Mother. Alessandra. I will see you at dinner." Simon bowed and left.

Alessandra sighed. "Your grace, I know..."

"Before you speak, let me say that whatever you tell me now will not leave this room. Not even the duke will be told, unless you wish it."

"Thank you, your grace."

"I also want to say that I will not force you into conversations if you feel uncomfortable or uneasy. But I am here to listen, if, and when, you feel ready to open up and surrender whatever inner sorrows that have you struggling each and every day. However, why you refuse to even tell your brother quite baffles me."

"I have told him very little, 'tis true. It will put him in a most awful rage. There are things...I will not risk his sanity, your grace. The fiendish spirits that control me will control him as well. In fact, they already have in some ways. He is just as unrested as I am because he watches over me. I have terrible dreams and need to be awakened. He has avoided going out and has taken to drinking brandy excessively. He is having much difficulty accepting my deformity." Alessandra looked down at her left hand, still covered by the lavender muff. "I can't blame him. It is most hideous."

"But there is more than just your hand, is there not?"

Alessandra bowed her head.

The duchess took hold of Alessandra's left hand and removed the gossamer covering. She carefully caressed the twice broken fingers.

"Well, I guess you should begin the telling of it then."

Alessandra looked at the duchess. Her bottom lip began to tremble. "I'm sorry, your grace. Please forgive me. It is just too difficult."

The duchess held Alessandra's hands in her own. "Don't ever apologize, dearest."

"I do not have one moment where I feel at peace. Even though I am free from Cecil, I am still bound to him. Sebastian and Simon think that I can just clear my mind of the events that have taken place. I cannot. I have tried, and tried, and tried. But the brutal torture and mental cruelty that has preyed upon me every second of every day is not erasable. During my marriage not one whisper did I use in protest of the treatment I received. For if I made the tiniest of sounds, I became the benefactor of even worse atrocities. I learned rather quickly to stifle my cries. Hold onto my screams. And shed no tears. As a reward for my acceptance and compliance, I was given jewels. But even then, cruelty was never far behind."

"When did it start, Alessandra? Was there not any sign before your marriage that he was of questionable character?"

"No. Just the opposite. He was very kind and charming up until our wedding night. He became different. Very withdrawn. Very...dark."

"Dark?"

Alessandra's hand twitched. She dabbed at her eyes when she stood to take a turn about the room.

The duchess remained seated, and silent, letting her troubled guest take whatever time needed to speak.

Alessandra sat back down on the settee. "He had me stand naked in the center of the room. All he did was walk around me in a continuous circle. Not once did he kiss me. Or touch me. It seemed like hours had passed before he told me to lie down. So I did. He followed me to bed, but kept his clothes on. He held my arms above my head with one hand around my wrists. I told him he was hurting me, but all he did was cackle. 'Don't fear my sweet' he said. 'It will all be over quickly.' Then with his other hand he took hold of my right..." Alessandra lowered her head and stared at her hands. "He squeezed so hard. I cried for him to stop, but he wouldn't. He held his hand up. Drops of blood were on his fingertips. He smiled. I asked him if he could please stop and he said I have no right to speak. He said I was his property now and I was his to do with as he pleased."

The duchess began to understand why no detail of the torture was not told before this day. She questioned her own decision to continue to listen.

"He bent his head then. Biting where his hand had been. I screamed. The pain was awful. I couldn't stop shaking. He told me I was disobeying his command to lie still and that he needed to teach me a lesson. A lesson he said that would also keep me from chasing other men. I told him I married him. I didn't want any other man. He bit me again. Viciously. I felt his teeth ripping my skin. When he lifted his face to look at me his lips were covered in blood. Just like his fingers. So much blood. He left me then. Our marriage was not consummated that night." Alessandra looked up. "I need to stop, your grace. I'm sorry, but I do not want to continue."

The duchess, who at first sat dignified, now fought back her own despondency.

"I need some air, your grace. I cannot breathe."

Both women walked out onto the balcony, arms

around each other. Time had passed as they stood in silence. How much, Alessandra did not know, but the sky had grown dark, and the grounds were quiet.

The duchess excused herself then, resigning to her chambers for the night. Alessandra remained behind, relishing the cold air, and watching the vapors as she exhaled.

The grounds were covered with patches of snow from the unusual weather that had enveloped England in recent weeks. Moon beams hugged the trees as crystalized snow glistened on the branches. It would have made a beautiful scene had her visit to Somersby been for a different reason than the one that brought her here.

Knowing that it would take more than the Christmas-like atmosphere to alleviate the cause for her journey, Alessandra turned to walk back inside and saw Simon standing in the doorway.

"You heard didn't you?"

Simon reached for her hand, brought it to his lips, and placed a gentle kiss upon each finger. The warmth of his hand enveloped the coldness of hers.

Alessandra thought to step back, but was held in place by Simon's tender touch. He caressed her fingers as though they were perfection, each one elegant and flawless.

"Tell me, Alessandra. Does your hand give you much pain when I touch it?"

"No more than whatever pain I already feel. Although some days are worse than others."

Simon didn't let go. His strong extremities covered hers. "Why didn't you send word? I would have come for you."

"Cecil had the butler show him my missives before they were sent out. I had no friends, no allies, no one to turn to. I was completely alone. I suppose if I tried hard enough I could have found a way. But fear...it is very controlling. And intimidating."

"What about your father? Did he not suspect the

cruelty to which you were subjected?"

"My father did not know. I did not *want* him to know. It would have destroyed him to learn that the match he arranged was a match with Satan."

"But your hand. Surely there was no doubt in his eyes that you were being abused?"

"He passed away prior to my hand being broken the first time. Any markings or bruises I received before he died were in the most concealed places. My husband thought himself to be quite the gentleman for his...discretion. It was soon after my father died that the abuse became worse. In fact, moments after the solicitor had left from reading the will, and explaining that all had been entailed to Sebastian, I encountered a most horrifying experience. Not one thing was left under Cecil's care."

"Except you."

"Except me."

Chapter Eighteen

"So, Mister Meade, what you are saying is that my wife's father left everything to his son."

"That is correct, sir. However, a yearly stipend has been set up for her. The late earl has also made very clear in his will that the estate could be entitled to another male descendent, but only if Sebastian Arthur Smythson, Earl of Ashleigh, passes on before he himself obtains an heir.

"I see. By another male descendent you are referring to a son born of my wife."

"Precisely."

Cecil's gaze shifted from the solicitor towards Alessandra. His eyes cold. The coldest she has ever seen them. And calculating. She knew, that one way or another, punishment awaited her.

"Well, my dear. We wouldn't want to risk having your father's estate not stay in the family, now would we?"

Alessandra's voice was weak. "No...of course not."

Cecil stood then, hurrying the exit of the solicitor. Alessandra heard the front door close. Her husband's footsteps more pronounced than usual. It was coming. She knew that torture was imminent. She held a subservient pose.

Cecil entered the library, locking the door behind him.

His stance minacious, he removed his cravat and carefully placed it on his desk.

"My dear, you look frightened. Why?"

"No reason, my lord."

"Do you speak the truth?"

"Yes, my lord."

"I don't believe you. You're hiding something from me. What is it?"

Alessandra felt a sharp pain across her cheek. The force from his slap pushed her off balance. She fell to her knees. A whimper escaped her lips.

"Do not ever show me your emotions. Ever!"

She received a kick to her ribs and screamed.

Cecil continued his rage. "You spoke to your father didn't you?" He turned his back. "You spoke to him and convinced him to keep me out of his will. You told him to give everything to your already wealthy brother. You did, didn't you? Answer me!"

Another kick.

Alessandra heard a crack. She panted to draw in air. The pain became more unbearable with each word she spoke.

"No...my...lord...I...did...no...such...thing."

"Then tell me why your father would do this. Why would he not want me to be the executor of your stipend?"

"My...lord..." Alessandra couldn't utter another syllable. Her eyes closed. She felt herself drift into blackness, only to be pulled out of it by her husband's fury.

Cecil knelt beside his wife, wrapping her now disheveled hair around his right hand, squeezing her cheeks with his left.

"So my sweet, what should we do? What should I do? You have no money. Well, you do, but it is under your brother's control. Perhaps we should finally consummate our marriage...hmm? Maybe get you with child? I'm sure Sebastian would be most generous once he learns his sister is in a certain way."

Alessandra did not answer. Her breaths were short and weak.

Cecil moved his hand from her face to her dress, ripping the material with one yank.

Alessandra sat up. She began to rock to and fro. Her arms hugging her drawn up knees. She heard footsteps approach her door and stop.

Please go away. Leave me be Cecil. Just leave me be.

"Alessandra. Are you alright? Can I come in?"

No. Stay away from me.

"Alessandra, it's me, Simon. Please let me come in."

Simon? Simon's here? No, it's a trick. He's not here. No one is here. No one except me. And Cecil.

Alessandra heard her doorknob turn. *Oh God. No more. Please no more.*

The door opened. Fearing the worst, Alessandra closed her eyes. The bed dipped. Hands grabbed her shoulders.

"Alessandra, it's me, Simon. You're dreaming."

She pushed his arms away.

Simon grabbed her again. "Alessandra! Open. Your. Eyes!"

His voice broke through her trance. Her eyes fluttered. She looked around the room.

"You're really here?"

"Yes, I'm really here."

"How?"

"Your brother informed me of your bad dreams. I thought it would be best to stay in the adjacent room. I'm glad I did."

"But you can't. It's not proper. The servants…"

"All are good people and very discreet. They will not surmise anything unjust or improper between us."

"You don't need…"

"Yes, I do. You're under my care, Alessandra. I promised your brother. I am not going anywhere."

"But the duke and duchess."

"I have already explained to them before your arrival of my plans. Why do you think your maid was given the room on the other side of yours?"

"My maid never hears me when I have night terrors."

Simon arched a brow.

"I know for a fact she cannot hear my cries at night."

"How do you know?"

Alessandra took hold of a pillow for comfort. "Sadly, I was not the only one graced with Cecil's violent attention." Alessandra cleared her throat. "Cecil hated, no he despised, anyone who did not follow orders exactly to his specifications. He used to scream that the female servants must be deaf since his demands were not completed as he instructed. Over time he discharged the entire staff, except his butler who had been with him for years. Edwin was just as nasty as Cecil. I always thought those two were born from the same seed. When Cecil replaced the staff, he only hired one female servant. That was Josie. Even the cook was male.

"One night I heard both Cecil and Edwin yelling at Josie. Cecil was in a terrible rage. I was afraid to leave my room, but I did anyway. When I got halfway down the stairs, I saw Josie lying on the floor, her hand covering her bloodied ear. I ran down the rest of the way and knelt beside her. Cecil pulled me away. He said she deserved to get a beating. When I asked him why, he said it was because she disobeyed his order that any missives I write do not get sent unless he reads them first."

Alessandra hugged the pillow closer to her chest. "You see...it was my fault she was slapped over and over again...on her ear...the side of her head. I had given her a missive. I asked her to send it for me the next time she was out running errands. But she never got the chance. Edwin must have overheard me talking to Josie and told Cecil. I'm to blame." Alessandra began to rock her body once more and whispered, "I'm to blame."

Simon's voice was quiet, full of melancholy. "You are

not to blame for your husband's depravity, Alessandra."

"Yes I am! You don't understand," Alessandra said. "That missive was addressed to *you*."

Simon's jaw clenched. "Alessandra..."

"Don't say anything, Simon. Please just go."

"At least tell me what you wrote in the missive."

"It matters not." Alessandra, feeling drained, threw the pillow to the floor and turned onto her side. "You can leave now." She waited until she heard the click of the door, and then cried herself into oblivion.

Simon listened outside Alessandra's door until her cries subsided, then made his way to the library, in which he now sat, brandy decanter half empty, staring at a closed book of Shakespearean sonnets. Next to that was a collection of poems by Lord Byron. The latter lay open to *She Walks in Beauty*.

Whenever sleep eluded him as it had this night, Simon always turned to his literary friends, William and George. Only this time, reading their words did not lull him, but stirred his emotions. In fact, Lord Byron had made him most aware of them. Hence, the need for brandy.

Simon rubbed his eyes as he saw a hint of sunlight beckon him. He stretched his arms, then legs, and carried Lord Byron's poems over to the window. Simon began to read again, finishing the last two lines aloud.

"*A mind at peace with all below,
A heart whose love is innocent.*"

He closed the book and threw it on a nearby chair. He leaned his head against the glass pane and closed his eyes. *Pray Alessandra, I know your mind has no peace. Not even in daylight. But if you will only trust me, I can be your peace.*

Chapter Nineteen

Simon jumped at the tap he felt on his shoulder. He turned, closed fist at the ready. "Jasper!" The marquess relaxed his boxing stance. "Sorry old man. What are you doing up at this hour?"

"It's morning, my lord. The chimes have rung eight times. The graces have already taken their meal and are out for an early ride."

"I take it then that breakfast awaits me? And eight, you say? I only just closed my eyes." Simon rolled his stiff neck from side to side, resulting in a most unpleasant crackling effect. Popping followed after he rolled his shoulders in a backward motion.

The butler grimaced at the sounds. "Are you not well, my lord?"

"I'm quite well, Jasper. I just didn't have...never mind. I'll be fine shortly." Simon continued to stretch and the butler continued to grimace. "Have a bath drawn. Come for me as soon as it's prepared."

"Yes, my lord." Jasper hesitated to move.

"Jasper?"

"I beg your pardon, my lord. May I have a word with you?"

"Certainly, Jasper." Simon began to exit the library.

The butler lagged behind. "Well, out with it Jasper."

"First, I want to apologize most emphatically, my lord, as I mean no ounce of disrespect."

"Jasper, I'm tired, I'm hungry, and I'm in no mood for riddles. Now what is it you wish to say?"

"It's Lady Drake, my lord."

"What about her? Where is she?"

"In the morning room, my lord."

Simon walked into the hallway. Footsteps abounded from servants attending to their duties.

"Please, my lord, it is most important."

Simon stopped outside the morning room. The smell of baked apples called to him, tempting his mouth. His stomach rumbled. He exhaled deeply before facing the butler.

"Jasper, if you do not hurry up and finish what you're trying to say, I will demote you to footman!"

"Yes, my lord. Well, you see, Lady Drake did not want me to pour her tea."

"And this is troubling to you, is it?"

"Yes, my lord. It is my duty to serve. But when I offered a second time and then a third time, she dismissed me."

"Is that what all this fidgeting with you is about? A cup of tea?"

"My lord, it is not right for Lady Drake to take on the duty of a servant."

"Ah, she scorned your pride, did she?"

"In a manner of speaking, my lord, yes. Yes, that's exactly how I feel. Mind you, I have nothing but admiration for Lady Drake. I remember her when she was nothing but a rambunctious little girl, only so high." Jasper held out his hand, palm down, at waist level.

"She means no harm, Jasper. I'm sure you can understand why she would have such a request."

"Yes, my lord, which is why I, and all the other servants, would consider it an honor to be at Lady Drake's disposal, day or night."

"Perhaps in time she will accept such kindness. But right now, just give her privacy. She has a maid and a maid is all she wants to assist her."

"Yes, my lord."

"Thank you, Jasper. You may go." The butler bowed. Simon gave a slight nod in return, and then entered the morning room.

Alessandra blew on her hot tea before sipping. Placing the delicate cup back on the saucer, she closed her eyes, contemplating going back to bed. But she knew there would be no rest for the weary. At least for her. Once her thoughts began, they didn't stop. Reliving a vicious and never ending stream of darkened memories was a continuous and constant battle.

"Good morning, Alessandra."

Oblivious to Simon's entrance, she sat up with a start.

He gave a small chuckle. "Sorry, I didn't mean to startle you."

"It's quite alright." Alessandra looked at his ragged state of undress. "You look...awful."

Simon raised a brow. "Thank you. I was going for that very effect. I'm sure Jasper thought so, too, although he didn't clearly state it. Thank goodness I didn't bring Oakes to Somersby. He would be having an apoplexy right about now."

"I'm sorry. That was rude of me." Alessandra moved her gaze from his stubbled face to his throat that was exposed, thanks to the absence of a cravat. She shifted her eyes a little lower, taking in the hint of dark hair protruding from undone buttons at the top of his shirt. Even though the once staunch fabric was now loose, she could still make out the line of his muscles with his every movement. Again, she silently thanked his lack of waistcoat and cravat.

She watched him still as he tried to control the unruly thick dark waves of his hair, but they only stood on end. His attempt to fix his mane was unattainable.

"Only tea this morning, Alessandra? Surely you do not wish to insult Cook by refusing to partake of this marvelous breakfast she has prepared?"

"I'm not very hungry."

"Hungry or not, you need to eat. You look unwell yourself, by the way. No doubt from having an uneasy night."

Simon walked over to the sideboard and filled two plates with sliced cooked apples sprinkled with cinnamon, toast, and poached eggs. He set one plate in front of Alessandra, her toast already buttered and smeared with blackberry jam.

"Thank you."

They sat in an awkwardness that neither one liked. Swallowing a bite of toast, Alessandra looked at Simon.

"Were you not able to sleep at all last night?"

"I fell asleep in the library." *Standing against the window, thinking of you.*

"I'm sorry if I startled you with my dream. They seem to come more frequent lately." Alessandra took another bite of toast.

"By the way, where is your maid?" Simon queried. "I thought you liked to have her close by in case you need any assistance."

"Sometimes. But today she is busy trying to repair some of my gowns that have become frayed at the hems."

"Those dreaded black gowns. You should not be wearing mourning clothes."

"Simon! My husband died."

"After what he did to you, he does not deserve your obedience to protocol. How long has he been expired anyway?"

"Nine months."

"You've worn mourning clothes long enough."

"The proper mourning period consists of at least two years with the first year and one day in black."

"Yes, for someone who deserves to be mourned. And he

does not."

"I won't go against propriety."

"We'll see. I'll have my father request that you come out of mourning. Although I'm sure my mother has already mentioned it to him. And you wouldn't want to go against a ducal order, would you? Besides, no one needs to know the truth about how long ago your husband died."

"Simon, do you hear yourself? You're being ridiculous."

"Am I? I don't think so. Unless of course that bad dream you had last night had nothing to do with your husband?"

Alessandra remained silent.

"I thought as much. I wouldn't believe you anyway if you told me different."

"Why?"

Simon swallowed before answering. "It scared me, Alessandra. To hear your fear. To see your fear. It was quite unnerving." Simon moved to the seat directly on Alessandra's right.

"The missive you wrote. The one you gave Josie to send. What did it say?"

"I don't think..."

"Please tell me, Alessandra. I want to know. I *need* to know."

Alessandra let out a breath, not realizing she had been holding it. "I wanted to come home. I wanted you to rescue me. I watched Cecil burn the letter. He did not open it. But his warning to me...and to Josie...was quite clear."

Simon shifted his body so that he fully faced Alessandra. Carefully, he turned her chair so she faced him as well. He took hold of her left hand and placed it on his knee. When she didn't pull it back, he touched her cheek, and moved his face closer to hers. His hand slid from her cheek to the back of her neck, his face even closer than before, lips almost touching.

"I am truly, truly, sorry."

She gave a small smile. "I know. So am I."

Before she knew what was happening, Simon lightly kissed her lips. Alessandra jerked her head back. "Why did you do that?"

"I beg your pardon. It just seemed right."

"You should not have done that, Simon."

"Forgive me. I meant no disrespect."

"I should go."

"Pray, do not leave."

"I think it is best."

"Best for whom? Do not be afraid of your feelings, Alessandra."

"But I *am* afraid. You're trying to awaken in me something; I don't know what to call it, except unfathomable emotions. I must never be alone with you after this."

Simon's jaw clenched. "Why ever not?"

"It's not appropriate! For heaven sakes, Simon, I am still in mourning!"

"I will not discuss your absurd allegiance to mourn the dead barbarian!"

Alessandra's chin quivered. "Get away from me!"

"Alessandra, I'm...I'm sorry. That was totally out of line. I don't know what came over me."

Alessandra pushed her chair back, forcing Simon to move as well. He caught her hand, but she pulled it from his grip and ran for the door. She turned, her eyes moist. "I'm sorry." Then she left.

Simon ran his hand through his hair. "Curses!"

At once, Jasper entered. "My lord?"

"What is it, Jasper?"

"Your bath is ready, my lord."

"It'll have to wait. Something else needs my urgent attention at the moment."

Chapter Twenty

Alessandra didn't return to her room but found herself outside in the garden. She paced back and forth over a section of the stone path that led from the entrance to an apple tree.

She turned on her heel, beginning a fourth turn down the same stone path, only to find her way blocked by Simon, still in his disheveled state, carrying a plate of food.

"I came to make sure you were well."

"I am fine. Thank you."

"I brought you your breakfast. You didn't finish it." Simon walked over to one of the small garden tables and set down the plate. "I didn't mean to make you feel uncomfortable earlier. I'm sorry."

"Don't Simon. Please don't."

"Don't what?"

"Don't apologize. It's me. Don't you understand? It's me."

"What are you talking about?"

"Simon, I am so confused. And I think you are, too."

"No. That's not true. The more I think about you, the more I become convinced that you belong to me. And then I become enraged at what has happened to you."

"It's pity, Simon. Nothing more."

"It's not pity, Alessandra."

"I don't think I can do this. I told you once I gave all my being to another man. I can't do it again."

"I will not hurt you like Cecil did if that is what has you so afraid. Please believe that."

"I do. But..."

"But what? I will not force you to do anything you do not want to do. I have such strong feelings for you. And I have *always* cared for you, Alessandra. Part of me wants to put a shield around you for protection and the other part wants to hold you. Love you."

Alessandra took a step back.

"Please, Alessandra. Do not shut me out. Do not be afraid of me."

"I *am* afraid. I was married to a monster, remember? A degenerate. A man who was cruel and who loved to play cruel games."

"And now he is dead."

"Dead, but he still lives on. In my mind, he lives on."

"You need to forget him. Begin a new life. That is why you came back to England, is it not? To leave your past and start again? You need someone who will give you that life. You need me."

"No."

"No to a new life? Or no to needing me?"

"No to everything. It is very complicated, Simon."

"Make it uncomplicated."

"It's not that simple."

"Explain it to me then."

"I do not want to tread into dangerous territory."

"Alessandra, there is so much more to life." Simon moved closer. His arms encircled her. His voice low as he drew her closer still. "And I know there is so much more about your marriage to Cecil. I am your friend first and foremost. But believe me when I say that I will make you forget him. In time, you will forget."

And then he let her go and walked away.

Chapter Twenty-One

Alessandra Journal Entry, Oxfordshire, 17 July 1816

My school girl annoyances have turned on me. I have a most determined shadow belonging to a six feet four inch marquess who follows me no matter where I go. How he put up with my undying devotion all those years ago I will never understand. I realize now why my brother resented my persistent presence. It's annoying!

Do not misunderstand me, dear journal, for I do like talking with the marquess. True, I have weaknesses, but I am not an invalid. Nor am I as feeble as he thinks I am, even though my biggest shortfall is an atrocious, somewhat unusable, unreliable, and most unattractive extension to which I am at the mercy for this horrid penmanship.

And of course, the night terrors. Those dreadful dreams that will not go away. I have not mentioned another word to the duchess or Simon about my marriage, or lack thereof, since it truly was not a marriage at all, but a metamorphosis. A metamorphosis that changed me from a vivacious young lady, who loved life, into a sullen broken spirit.

Even if there comes a day when I am at ease in discussing my tortured life, will the marquess truly accept the person I have become?

He has promised that he will make me forget the sadistic creator of my transformation. But that, I'm afraid, will never happen. How can it when my own physically altered being is an interminable reminder of the wretchedness in which I lived?

Worse still, there is one event for which I am solely guilty. It is one that causes me tremendous grief and insurmountable emotional distress. Would I dare speak of it even if I could? The child I lost? The child I could not protect? Will God ever forgive me for doing the unforgivable?

Chapter Twenty-Two

Smythson House, London, 8 August 1816

Sebastian picked his head up off his desk and moaned. His arms ached from being outstretched before him. The last thing he could remember was receiving a missive from Simon. After that was a complete blur.

He turned his head from side to side; all the while his moans growing louder from the continuous pounding in his head. He sat up enough to grab his head with his hands.

He heard what sounded like crinkling paper and realized he had passed out on top of the crumpled note. He inched his way to a full sitting position and grabbed the wrinkled ball, only to find that he wished he burned it after reading it the first time.

Sebastian,

First, I will begin this letter with some reassurance. Your sister is in good hands. She is never out of my immediate vicinity and is receiving enough attention to keep her from being a total recluse, yet she still has her periods of privacy where she can let go of her tears without humiliation. We would never chastise her for showing those tears, but your sister was always one for propriety.

Second, and most importantly, she has given some details. I dare say there is an abundance more she is not conveying to us, but the little she has shared reveals a marriage most scurrilous from the onset.

Which brings me to the subject of her night terrors. I never quite understood the full capacity of the fear you explained to me until I experienced it myself. There are no words I could scribe that would explain the absolute panic on her face when she is in the throes of them. I cringe at the mere thought of seeing her so.

But do not worry, my friend. She is with people who love her dearly. We will do whatever it takes to rid her mind and spirit of the evil dead beast that haunts her night and day. I give you my word.

Your friend,
Simon

Sebastian wadded the crinkled paper back up into a tight ball and threw it, watching it land next to the full crystal decanter on a nearby side table. Brandy, his own personal demon of late.

His eyes immediately fixed on the set of matching crystal snifters and licked his lips. Sweat formed above his brow and his hands started to shake. He was proud of himself before this night. Once Alessandra left for Somersby, Sebastian swore off touching any liquor. But upon reading the marquess' note, the familiar craving hit him full force. He tried to ignore it, and believed he had conquered the guilty thirst when he fell asleep while reviewing his estate books.

He woke a short time later, still haunted by the news that his sister's nightmares remained a fixture in her life. He pulled two bottles of brandy out from where he had hid them, emptied one into the decanter, and used the other one to drink himself into a stupor.

Now, after reading the missive again, he no longer could control the urge to quench his thirst. He slid the back of his hand across his dry lips. He rose from his leather chair and stepped towards the side table. "Just one more drink, God. Just let me take but one more."

Chapter Twenty-Three

Somersby, Ducal Country Estate, Oxfordshire, 14 August 1816

Simon watched Alessandra walk with her maid and Oliver towards the of field of red poppies. The marquess did not learn much about the boy from Alessandra, except that he was Josie's son. When he questioned his staff, Oliver was called an intelligent child, but like all young boys his age, he was quite fond of practical jokes; to which Simon recently became aware himself after finding a frog sitting on top of his desk.

Hearing giggles coming from behind a leather chair, Simon exaggerated shock and horror as best he could, scrunched his nose and shrieked for help. When Jasper bolted into the library, Oliver could not contain himself. His giggles expanded into bouts of uncontainable gaiety. When Simon added to the ruckus, Jasper rolled his eyes and curtly left.

That was when Simon knew. He knew there were no doubts about his feelings for Alessandra. He knew this was what he wanted. This mayhem of mirth and amusement to fill his own estate of Heavensford. And to have Alessandra as the mother of such glorious jocularity.

When Simon turned to talk with the boy, Oliver fled the library in a flash. No doubt afraid he would be scolded should his mother find out.

Voices from across the field interrupted Simon's thoughts, compelling him to re-focus his vision back on the present scene.

"Oliver, don't go too far ahead of us. Oliver!"

The boy didn't stop. His little legs picked up speed as he ran with his head down, arms stretched out as if he were soaring like a bird, which in turn made him oblivious to the huge boulder that was a short distance away.

Simon saw the danger and knew the women would not be able to catch up to the boy. The marquess quickly bounded. He made a beeline towards the front of the massive rock, hoping to cut the child off before he made contact. But Oliver turned at the last second and headed down the slope, missing the boulder completely.

The women stopped their pursuit and grabbed each other's hands once they saw Simon. But their relief was short-lived. They watched the marquess continue his chase.

Simon's long legs quickly caught up to Oliver, but before he could grab hold, the boy dropped to his belly and rolled to the bottom of the hill.

Simon stopped halfway down.

"Oliver! Come here, lad."

The boy didn't move.

"Oliver! Now!"

Running as fast as his legs could take him, Oliver raced to where Simon stood. His light brown eyes looked up at the marquess.

"Yes, my lord?" Oliver shifted his stance in nervous anticipation, fearing Simon's silence was a precursor to punishment. His voice was barely above a whisper. "My lord? Should I find a switch?"

"Why would you need to find a switch?"

"I didn't listen to my mum when she wanted me to stop

running."

Curious to find out more, Simon asked, "Have you been hit before, Oliver?"

Oliver bent his head. "Yes, my lord. But only because I needed it."

Simon kept an aloof expression so as not to frighten Oliver more than he already was. He knelt down before him.

"Tell me the truth, lad. Who hit you?"

"I'd rather not say, my lord."

"Oliver, it is important that I know. Do you understand that I care what happens to you?"

Oliver, his head still down, looked at his feet that couldn't keep still. "I was sworn not to tell anything, my lord. I can't break a promise."

"Were you hit here at Somersby or while in America?"

"Oh, not here, my lord. Everyone is very nice here. It was before we sailed on the ship."

Simon, not fully satisfied with the boy's response, questioned him again.

"Was it your mum that hit you?"

"No, my lord. It was a man."

"A man? But you can't tell me who the man was? Did this man come to England with you?"

"No, my lord. He died."

Cecil. Simon placed his hands on Oliver's shoulders. "Look at me, lad."

Oliver peered at the marquess with apprehension.

"You will not be hit. Do you understand? You will have a punishment for disobeying your mother, but it will not involve getting hit with a switch. I don't believe in hitting a young child."

"What about a lady, my lord?"

"Especially not a lady."

Oliver wanted to trust Lord Bevan. "Do you promise, my lord?" he asked him.

"Absolutely."

"Then Lady Drake can stop crying now. She cries all the time, my lord. My mum cries, too, sometimes. But now I can tell them they don't have to be afraid anymore."

"You do that, Oliver." Simon turned away from him, but stayed on his knees. "How would you like to get a piggyback ride up to the house? Then after lunch I'll teach you to skip pebbles across the lake."

"Really? Oh thank you, my lord!"

The marquess and Oliver started up the hill, both laughing as they passed the maid. Then Simon's gaze collided with Alessandra's eyes. *There is much we need to discuss, my sweet. But all in due time.*

Chapter Twenty-Four

Simon kept his promise and took Oliver down to the lake after lunch to skip pebbles. Once there, the boy insisted that he'd rather search for frogs.

"Why do you like frogs so much Oliver?"

"I just like them. Plus they scare girls."

"Yes, I guess that's a good reason to like frogs. Do you always try to scare people with your frogs?"

"It's fun, my lord. But my mum doesn't think so. She hates it when I put frogs in the laundry basket. It scares her, you see. You know, when they jump at her. But I guess that's because she's a girl and not a boy."

"I suppose so."

"You're not scared of frogs, are you my lord?"

"Not at all."

"I don't think Jasper likes them."

"Jasper is a busy man, Oliver. He keeps things tidy. A frog belongs outside, not in the house."

"Yes, my lord."

"Oliver, when you were running earlier today, did you not see the boulder? You could have been seriously hurt. Your mother would have been quite upset."

"I saw the big rock. I knew to turn and run the other way."

"But why did you not stop when your mother called your name?"

"I was flying, my lord."

"Oliver..." Simon didn't know how to continue. He never had a conversation with a young boy before. "How old are you, Oliver?"

"Six, my lord."

"You articulate very well for a boy of six. Especially one who is a servant's child."

"The lady teaches me, my lord."

"Which lady?"

"Lady Drake, my lord. She said all boys need to learn to enunciate properly if they want to become fine gentlemen."

"Doesn't your mother teach you your subjects?"

"Of course, my lord. But Lady Drake likes to help."

"That's very kind of her."

"She *is* rather nice. And lovely, too, my lord."

"Indeed she is."

"Do you like Lady Drake, my lord?"

"Very much."

"Do you want to marry her?"

"What do you know about marriage, you little scamp?"

"Well...I heard mum and Lady Drake talking, my lord. They thought I was asleep, but I was only pretending."

"I see. What did you hear Lady Drake say?"

"She told my mum that you want to make her happy, but she's afraid. Do you, my lord? Do you want to make Lady Drake happy?"

"I want everyone to be happy, Oliver."

"Will you help Lady Drake not be afraid, my lord?"

The marquess was taken aback by the seriousness of the conversation. To have a six year old converse with such an authoritative tone sent shivers down Simon's spine. Only one thing could make a young child ask such questions with allegiance to protect. *Experience with someone who was not of honorable character.*

"Oliver...lad...I want to help Lady Drake and I promise I will do my best to not make her cry. Alright?"

Oliver shifted his body so that his frame stood at attention. Fist closed, he motioned Simon with his pointer finger to bend down. The marquess obliged the boy.

"Yes, Oliver?"

"If I tell you things, my lord, you mustn't let Lady Drake know I told you. Or my mum."

"What kind of things, lad?"

Oliver whispered. "Bad things, my lord."

Simon felt the hair on the back of his neck stand on end. He reached out his hand. Oliver took hold.

"Don't worry, Oliver. I won't tell. Whatever you wish to say will be our secret."

"Oliver!"

Simon and Oliver turned around. Standing behind them was Alessandra.

"Um...good afternoon, Lady Drake."

"Oliver, go to your mother. She's up in the school room. It's time for you to practice your reading."

"Yes, my lady." Oliver bowed. Then faced Simon and bowed again. "Goodbye, my lord. Thank you for everything."

"Goodbye, lad." Simon waited until the boy was a good distance away before turning towards Alessandra. "Oliver's very intelligent, is he not?"

"Very."

"I think he will make a fine gentleman someday, Alessandra. A fine gentleman, indeed."

Chapter Twenty-Five

Simon took Alessandra's hand firmly, not allowing her to pull it back as he motioned towards the summerhouse. She didn't move. Neither spoke for a moment. Then Alessandra slowly nodded, permitting the marquess to escort her to their favorite childhood excursion.

Even though the edifice held only one room, it was vast and accommodating. The outside was surrounded by Gallica roses and Honeysuckle bushes. The upkeep was obviously no less important than the rest of Somersby.

All four sides of the structure were done in glass so as not to obstruct the view from inside. Alessandra had forgotten the magnificent scenery from long ago.

The furniture had been changed. No longer were there basic wooden benches that Alessandra remembered. Instead an oversized chaise covered in rich fabric filled the center of the room. She took note to the side table ornamented with candles and the draperies that hung in the corners, waiting to be pulled closed for privacy when wanted.

Alessandra looked at Simon, his muscular figure encompassing a good portion of the entry. She watched him watching her. Her skin tingled. She didn't want it to tingle. She wanted no reaction to the man who stood before her.

Simon stepped forward away from the entrance. He crossed to the back wall and opened two additional glass panels, creating a breeze that swept the scent of honeysuckle and other foliage through the summerhouse.

Alessandra noticed a small bookcase, three shelves high against a side wall. "Books? Since when are there books in your parents' summerhouse?"

Within four strides Simon was behind her. His whisper warm upon her ear. "This is all for you, Alessandra."

She turned to face him, lifting her gaze to meet his. "For me? Why?"

"To help give you solace away from the manor. Away from the servants. And away from me. Although the last I hope is never a reason you come here."

"It's lovely. Thank you." Alessandra spied a basket behind the chaise. "Is that a picnic basket? How?"

"I had Cook prepare it. I was hoping to talk you into walking down here with me later, but your unexpected presence to chase Oliver home took care of my request."

"Indeed."

"As soon as you are in need of sustenance, just say the word and I will be most happy to lay out what I'm sure will be a small feast, if I know Cook."

Alessandra smiled, then watched the marquess walk around the summerhouse, hands clasped behind him.

"Remember when we used to come here when we were younger?" Simon asked her. "You, Sebastian, and myself? That was a fun time. No worries, no complications. Just good friends enjoying our youth."

"You may have enjoyed my company, but Sebastian didn't. He abhorred my very existence, you know."

"That's not true. He may have thought you a bit demanding in your quest to have my undivided attention, but he was a good sport nevertheless. I daresay he behaved like any other young man who had a sister, who in turn wanted to be noticed by her brother's most handsome friend."

"I suppose," Alessandra said in a somber tone. "There are days when I think back to when my father arranged for our journey to America. I wonder if I wasn't such a nuisance to Sebastian would he have talked my father into letting me stay in England. I truly did not want to go, but no one would listen to me. I begged my father every minute of the day to leave me behind. When he refused to listen to my ranting, I beseeched Sebastian to speak on my behalf. But he refused to listen to me as well. He said it was all for the better. He would be too busy running our father's estate and other holdings to have time for my care."

Alessandra walked to the entrance and leaned back against the door frame, letting the cool breeze touch her face. When she heard no movement from Simon, she continued. "I had written a letter to your mother. But then you know about that, do you not? Sebastian must have truly thought I would have complicated his life. I would have never expected my brother of disposing that letter had I not seen him take it myself. I never confronted him about that missive, at least not until the night of that dreadful dinner to which you were invited. It seemed that any attempt I put forth to stay in England was pointless."

She briefly looked at Simon, then turned her head back towards the scenery outside. "I gave up all hope. The journey to Savannah was a very long and quiet one."

Alessandra stepped out of the summerhouse, picked a rose, and began to walk towards the lake.

Simon followed. He kept his distance until Alessandra stopped walking. Only when he reached her side did he speak.

"I would have done everything in my power to keep you here. I hope you know that. I didn't know about a missive to my mother until Sebastian told me what he had done. And if the duchess would have received it, believe me, she would have travelled on horseback herself to the harbor in order to stop your father from taking you away."

"I know. Your mother treated me as if I was her own daughter. Sometimes I wish I were."

"Nay, don't wish that."

"Why ever not?"

"Because then it would be most criminal of me to do this." Simon tilted Alessandra's face up towards his and gently covered her lips with his own.

Chapter Twenty-Six

Simon pulled back, searching Alessandra's face for a reaction. He wasn't sure what kind exactly. Rejection perhaps? When he saw none, he pulled her closer, keeping one hand against her back as the other lightly caressed her cheek. He felt both her hands touch his hair, hesitant, but only for a moment.

"May I ask you a question, Simon?"

"Ask anything you wish."

"Why have you not married?"

The marquess chuckled. He relaxed his hold.

"Why does my question amuse you? I am being most sincere."

"I have no response for you, except that I thought about it. Once."

"Why only once? Was there no one worthy of your asking?"

"Oh, yes, sweet one. There was."

"What happened?"

"When I realized how much I cared for her, how much I wanted her as my wife, it was too late."

A dark cloud unexpectedly appeared, casting a shadow upon where they stood. A droplet bounced off Alessandra's nose. A loud boom sounded off in the distance. Another drop of rain fell. Then another, heavier than the first two. Several more followed in pursuit. "Oh! We need to get back to the manor." She spun away from Simon.

The marquess grabbed Alessandra's hand. "We're too far from the manor. The summerhouse is much closer."

They ran towards the glass structure. Simon holding Alessandra close to his side, directing her path to keep her from falling. By the time they reached their destination their clothes were soaked through.

Once inside, Simon closed the entrance doors, shutting out the massive downpour. The back panels were left ajar, allowing the sound of the heavily beaded moisture to be heard dancing on the surrounding foliage.

The marquess removed his dark blue waistcoat and white cravat and laid them in a corner. He looked at Alessandra. "I suggest you take your wet things off, my sweet, or you'll catch cold." Simon sat on the chaise and removed his black hessian boots and stockings. He began to roll up the bottom of his trousers when he noticed Alessandra had not moved, still wearing her clothes that were dripping wet.

"The duchess will not forgive me if I bring you back to the house shivering and sneezing."

"I...I'm...I'm fine," she said.

"You are not fine. Your teeth are chattering."

Alessandra squealed when Simon reached for her.

"Oh for heaven's sake, Alessandra, you don't need to get naked, but I believe losing your saturated gown and hosiery will be most beneficial to your health."

"And what...pray tell...do you wish me...to cover myself with?"

"There's a blanket in the chest by the bookcase. I'll get it for you."

Simon returned, holding up the luxurious covering. "I promise not to look. Remove your gown and when you're done, take hold of the blanket."

"I n...need help with the b...buttons."

"Indeed? It must be my lucky day."

"S...Simon!"

"I'm sorry. I couldn't resist. Turn around and I'll undo the buttons."

"What if...someone...sees us? This whole...edifice...is nothing...but glass."

"I don't think anyone is out in this weather. But to put your mind at ease, our exposure to others is a minor detail that I will quickly fix." Simon dropped the blanket onto the chaise and walked around the perimeter of the summerhouse, closing the draperies across the floor to ceiling glass petitions. The room darkened to almost black. Simon lit one of the candles on the side table by the chaise.

"Now, where were we? Ah, yes, your buttons." He stood behind Alessandra and began to unfasten the back of her gown. He saw the tip of a scar. Opening the gown further, he touched her chemise, feeling the welt through the thin fabric. "Who did this to you?"

Alessandra quickly pulled away, turning her back away from Simon's uncomfortable perusal.

"I can...slide the gown off...now. Thank...thank you."

"Tell me now, Alessandra. How did you get that scar? And do not say you have no wish to discuss it."

"It was...an accident."

"That's one lie. Pray, do not lie to me again."

Alessandra heard the controlled rage in Simon's voice. Knowing it was not meant for her, but for the dead beast who gave her the scar, she replied, "I locked...the door."

"What?" Simon thought he heard wrong. "You locked the door so you deserved that? Come here."

She walked towards Simon. Her eyes would not look into his, but down at his clenched fists.

"Turn around."

She did as he requested.

Simon pushed the gown off her shoulders, letting it fall in a puddle at her feet. He touched her scar again, tracing it through the thin fabric of her chemise as he did just a moment before. When he reached the end of the scar, he noticed another which began below it, but in a perpendicular direction. Across that was yet another scar.

"Alessandra, these are markings from a riding crop, are they not?"

"Y...yes."

Simon touched her shoulders, gently gliding his fingertips along the edge of her undergarment. He leaned into her and lightly kissed the back of her neck. Not knowing what to say, he stepped back, allowing Alessandra to wrap herself in the blanket. When she was done, Simon laid her next to him on the chaise. He blew out the candle and held her in his arms, wondering how he would be able to keep his promise to her; knowing that for the first time in his life, his power as a marquess was useless. His heart began to ache at the realization that he was very wrong. He now knew without a doubt that no matter how much time passes, no matter how much he tried to rid her mind of the past eight years, Alessandra would never be able to forget her dead husband.

Chapter Twenty-Seven

Alessandra burrowed herself into Simon, welcoming his warmth, his strength, and most of all, feeling of protection. The cocoon, in which she now found herself, was one she wished she had all along. A cocoon that should have been hers; that was in the making to be hers before the passing of her mother.

Reliving such dreams and hopes of what could have been and what should have been were frivolous at the moment, for Alessandra knew the past had been set, leaving her with the everlasting contemplation that should she allow Simon to embody her present, if she permitted him access to all of her being, to all of her heartache from the last eight years, would he truly be able to suspend her nightmares of the evil she was victim to in the present? Ultimately, would he be able to create a future where she would be able to live in total abandon of such unrelenting terror? If so, would she be able to accept it fully without fear?

Alessandra turned to face Simon. She knew she needed to explain to him the details of her scars. No, not just needed, but wanted. After seeing the few scars on her back, he didn't run. He didn't cringe at the ugliness of her hand. She wondered if he would be as accepting of the one unforgivable act that she herself had caused and would he still find her deserving of happiness?

Thoughts coming full speed, she wished she had her journal. It was her one solace. To unleash her thoughts on paper gave her the strength to survive another day.

Alessandra inched her way off the chaise and walked over to the glass panel by the bookcase. She opened the heavy drapery to let in some light and immediately spied a small basket holding an ink bottle and some quills. Upon further inspection she found that the bookcase not only contained various literary works, but blank tablets as well.

This is all for you, Alessandra. Simon's words echoed in her mind. She looked over at his sleeping form and studied the rise and fall of his chest. "So peaceful," she whispered. "If only I could find that peace for just one night."

Alessandra turned back towards the tablets and noticed that there was a title written on each cover in Simon's hand. *Dreams. Memories. Love.* Holding the books, she moved her still damp gown off the tufted corner chair and sat down.

She opened the book marked *Dreams*. Inside was a note on the first page.

Dearest Alessandra,

This journal is for all that your heart desires. My own dream is for you to be at peace. To once again live in happiness. To never fear life.

You alone are my one and only dream.
Simon

Next she opened the journal titled *Memories*. Again there was a note.

To My Constant Shadow,

Years ago you were never far behind and always enchanted me with your smile. My fondest memories are

your laugh, your scent... YOU!
Simon

Alessandra wiped a tear from her cheek and closed the journal. She took another look at Simon, wondering what message she would find in the book designated as *Love*. She turned the cover to reveal the first page.

My Sweet Alessandra,
I think of love, I think of you. I speak of love, I say your name. I wish for love, I wish for you.
Always know that my heart beats for you. Forever and always.
Simon

Alessandra closed the tablet and held it tightly against her bosom. She thought about the words written inside each journal, wanting to believe Simon was sincere. Knowing she needed to trust him.

She reached into the basket of ink and quills, opened the journal titled *Dreams* and began to write.

It is my dream, dearest journal, that I have the courage to accept all that has been done for me. The renovation inside this summerhouse that was a favorite childhood getaway was all done for me. The visit to Somersby was requested to help me. But was it because of the pain the marquess knew I must have received at the hands of the beast? Or was it done out of guilt, out of bereavement that he, Simon Thane Bevan, and everyone around him, could have helped to prevent such sadistic actions from happening?

Whatever his reasoning, I need to learn to trust this man who is willing to lay his heart before me. To deny his offer of acceptance of who I now am, a woman disfigured from years of torment, a woman forever scarred, is in fact to deny myself of the happiness to which the marquess has promised he would bring to my life.

Help me, dearest journal, to embrace the decision to allow Simon into my world. To let him emancipate me from the unequivocal madness that controls my nights as well as my days. To let him be the creator of my new life. And to give him the undeniable affection that I know he wants, and that I so deservedly long to have reciprocated back to me.

If only one dream comes true, Simon Thane Bevan, I dream that it's my trust in you.

Chapter Twenty-Eight

Lord, her touch ignites me! Simon clenched his teeth as he felt Alessandra's hand skim over his shirt, finding a place to rest above his heart. Then to his surprise, she moved her hand to lie directly against his heated skin. He welcomed her curious expedition.

The marquess remained still when she moved once again, this time losing the blanket altogether that until this moment, kept the feel of her body guarded from his gaze, and his touch.

Knowing he couldn't keep still much longer, he pulled her closer, feeling her breath exhale onto his now exposed chest.

He leaned his head to rest on top of hers, smelling the jasmine that her maid infused into her hair. The scent reminded him of the first time Alessandra had used it. She had just turned fifteen and was a guest at Somersby with her mother.

Simon had been leaving to return to London when their paths crossed in the corridor. She politely curtsied, wished him a safe journey, and walked into the music room to play a new piece for his mother that she learned on the pianoforte. Simon remained in that same spot, inhaling the scent of jasmine that lingered long after

Alessandra had left him standing behind. He was entranced by the scent then, and even more so now.

He shifted his body so as to lie directly facing Alessandra. Tilting her chin up to gaze at her green eyes with golden flecks, he ever so tenderly caressed her bottom lip with his thumb. Her lips parted slightly, exhibiting the tip of her tongue which barely, yet seductively, touched his finger. Such a small gesture, but one that he knew was difficult for her to relinquish so freely.

Simon took hold of her left hand and kissed the wedding band he had placed on her finger only hours before. "My dearest Marchioness, Alessandra Willow Bevan, wife of Marquess Simon Thane Bevan, Warrior of Heavensford and Protector of all who reside within it, are you happy?"

"Very, very happy."

"No regrets, my sweet one?"

"No regrets."

Simon pulled her closer into his embrace, holding her tightly, ensuring she knew without a doubt that there was no longer anything to fear. She was his. Body and soul. Just as he was now hers.

A cool breeze tickled his nose. Feeling the chill in the air increasing, he reached for the elaborate wedding quilt in the darkened chamber, a gift from his mother. But his fingers couldn't find it.

The marquess quietly left the bed, only to find his feet hit the floor with a thud, and more quickly than he anticipated. "What the...?" He rubbed his eyes as he looked around the room and realized he was not in his bed chambers, but instead in the glass paneled summerhouse. Alone. "A dream. Nothing but a dream."

Simon dragged a hand through his hair, wondering how long Alessandra had been gone. He found his Hessian boots in the dim light that was remaining of the day and quickly pulled them on. He noticed an array of books scattered upon the floor and the smudges on the side of the inkwell. His eyes scanned the top shelf. The journals were gone. In their place was a piece of folded paper, torn from one of the tablets. The marquess briskly opened it.

Simon,

I hope you will be able to decipher my words as not only are they difficult for me to script, but I am looking at them through streaming tears of confusion.

The journals you have given me have touched my heart. You have made your feelings quite clear. I so want to believe in you. In us. But there is so much I would need to tell you in order for you to fully accept me as I am. Are you truly capable, and without a doubt, certain beyond belief that you want to engage your heart in someone who might not be able to give back what you yourself are putting forth?

There is a blemish on my soul, you see. One that cannot be erased. Do I dare tempt fate and explain to you what it is? Or do I leave it residing in the recesses of my mind to fester day after day, night after night.

Would you run and hide from me, or would you live up to your moniker of Warrior and Protector?

I beg your forgiveness that I lost all courage in facing you when you awoke, but rather took the coward's way out and left when the opportunity presented itself. I will say this, Simon Thane Bevan, you were, are, and always will be the only one who can truly save me.

But can I, no...will I, allow my heart to beat for you as yours beats for me? I am too afraid to relinquish the depths of my soul.

I lived in an evil place, dearest Simon. I have done an evil thing. Would I curse your name with scandal should my black mark be found out? I would not be able to live another second, take another breath, if I brought any dishonor upon you and your family. I beg you with all my being, would you be absolutely willing and truly capable of helping me break away from the monstrosities that keep me chained to the spawn of Satan?

If you are still of the mind that you believe you can save me, then do so, Simon Thane Bevan, Warrior of Heavensford, and Protector of all who reside within it. Save me!

Alessandra

Simon bent his head, touched his fingertips to his lips, then gently touched her final words. *Save me!*

Chapter Twenty-Nine

Alessandra looked up when she heard the tapping on her chamber door. "He's here," she whispered to the empty air around her. She wasn't expecting Simon to follow her right away.

Yes, she told him to save her, but as he knocked again, Alessandra wondered if she really did want him to be at her side. Was she ready to face her fears and accept his rescue just as she asked him if he was ready to save her? She sat in silence, afraid to answer the light tapping that she knew would not stop until she did so.

Biting her bottom lip, she rose from the pillow she had been sitting on upon the floor. To the side was her trinket box, opened to convey the tiny silver thimble the marquess had gifted her years before.

Resting her forehead against the door for a moment, she silently tried to subdue her nerves. She turned the key, moving away from the door just in time for Simon's massive frame to enter. Alessandra returned to where she had been sitting.

The marquess closed the door behind him. "You left the summerhouse."

"I did."

The marquess looked down at the mahogany object.

"May I ask what is in the box?"

"Little gifts from long ago that I was able to keep hidden from Cecil."

"Why did you have to hide them? Surely he could not have thought gifts from your childhood would be a cause for alarm?"

Alessandra looked up. "He became enraged at the tiniest of things. A word regarding the weather from a passerby would even bring horrible consequences. Cecil was an extremely jealous man. It was nothing for him to destroy every tidbit of happiness I might have. There is one gift in particular that would have brought dire consequences had he found it."

"What might that be?"

Alessandra reached into the small box and pulled out the silver thimble. "This." She held it up, allowing candlelight to reflect off the shiny object. "He would have thought it a challenge that you called yourself my warrior."

"Well, then. Thank goodness he's already dead."

Alessandra jerked her hand back that was holding the thimble.

"I'm sorry. I should not have said that."

Placing the thimble back in the box, Alessandra reproached the marquess. "It's becoming quite a habit of yours, my lord. Constantly telling me how happy you are that I am a widow shows your lack of honorable character. I live with the markings, remember? I know he deserved to be gone from this earth."

"I am not happy you are a widow at such a young age, Alessandra. Do you honestly think I would want you to be?" His question was met with a shrug of her shoulders. Simon continued. "But I am glad that your most torturous husband is in the ground where he belongs. Tell me, do you ever think or wonder if there were other girls, other vulnerable young ladies he victimized? From what I have learned so far of this creature, I guarantee you that you were most likely not his first."

"Yes, I have wondered. In the beginning I wondered every day. But then I stopped wondering altogether, because I knew it would not do me any good. I needed to forget about other possible pawns in Cecil's sadistic games in order to survive. Mentally, I needed to lose myself. Can you understand that? Does that make me a horrible person because I worried about myself and no one else?"

"No, it does not. It makes you a victim trying to stay alive. You were a target for his malicious ways. An innocent girl who your husband recognized as easy prey. So no, Alessandra. You were not and are not a horrible person." Simon reached out his hand. "Enough of this. Come. I want to show you something."

Taking her hand, Simon guided Alessandra through the connecting door of their chambers and seated her in the leather chair by his writing table.

The aroma of musk and sandalwood enveloped her. *His* scent. She wrapped her arms in a self-embrace.

"Are you cold?"

"A little. It's a bit damp in here from the rain."

"Forgive me." Simon retrieved the top quilt from his bed and draped it over Alessandra's shoulders. "The fire in your room was burning nicely. I should not have pulled you from its warmth." He rubbed her cold hands. "We can go back."

"No!" Alessandra realized she asserted herself too offhandedly. She tendered her voice. "I mean no, I'm quite fine."

"I don't usually like my personal rooms overly heated, so I will have to remember…"

"It's alright." Alessandra looked around the room, her eyes averting the very masculine four poster bed. "What did you wish to show me?"

Simon took the cherry wood box off his dressing table and held it before her.

"What is this?"

"It's me."

Alessandra looked inside the box. A hint of jasmine caught her off guard. "That's my scent. How...?"

"Your gifts. I kept them. The bit of fabric where you embroidered our initials. The lock of hair you asked me to remember you by. There are other items I've kept, but these two are my most prized possessions. This box...it's what I am. It's *who* I am."

"And just who are you, Simon?"

"I am yours. Your every hope, your every wish. Whatever you desire. I will be that...I *am* that...and more."

Alessandra curled her legs up underneath herself and pulled the covering tighter around her body. The heavy scent of musk and sandalwood became more pronounced the more she fell into the warmth of Simon's quilt. She closed her eyes.

"It is getting late and you are tired. I should not have disturbed you."

Alessandra's eyes remained closed as she answered. "True, it has been an eventful day, but I'm not too tired to talk. Although I do seem to be making myself quite comfortable, would you not agree?"

"I believe I like having you in my chair. I can get adoringly accustomed to seeing you in that very spot every night."

Alessandra looked up at the marquess. "You had asked me once, nay a few times, to trust you. To let you help me forget what I so wrongly had been subjected to living."

"I read the note you left me at the summerhouse. Your trust will not be misplaced, Alessandra."

"You do understand that I have very little of that, if any, to give."

Simon took hold of her hands. "I believe you have more trust in me than you realize, or more than you are willing to admit."

"It matters not how much I have in me to give you, Simon. The truth is I cannot partake in this, for lack of a better word, excursion, if you find me unworthy."

Simon's features turned solemn. "You have stated in your letter that you have done an evil thing. Pray tell, what is this evil thing to which you refer? I cannot fathom that you would have one seed of evil or vileness in you."

"You speak without knowledge, Simon. Looks can be deceiving. I know that more than anyone."

"Your self-condescension is most disheartening, sweet one." Simon knelt before her, still holding her hands. "Look at me, Alessandra. Truly look at me. Search my eyes. Do you not believe me when I say that I am all things for you? That my heart beats for you?"

"No."

"Why not? I am here before you." Simon touched her cheek and wiped away the single tear with his thumb. "Do not be afraid. Give me whatever trust you have. Give me your soul as I beg you to take hold of mine. Every dark secret you have been hiding needs to be released, Alessandra. Do not let them control your faith in me any longer. Do not let him, the one who damaged you, have control over you any further. Let me in, sweet angel. Let me in." The last he whispered upon her ear.

"Oh, Simon." Alessandra fell into the marquess' waiting arms. "Hold me. Just hold me."

Simon took hold of this once innocent, now tormented girl, and held her as tightly as his arms would allow. "Cry to your heart's content, my sweet. I promise...everything will be alright." He touched her face. "Every dream and night terror you have are now mine, just as you are mine. Always and forever...you are mine."

Chapter Thirty

Simon cradled Alessandra in his arms until her weeping ceased. He was tempted to place her on his bed, but knew that he already mocked propriety by giving Alessandra the connecting room when she first arrived at Somersby. In fact, what she did not know was that her room had just been remodeled into a bedchamber. It was originally Simon's personal study; one that was necessary if he wanted a quiet place to work away from any visiting guests during his sojourns to the ducal estate. As soon as he contemplated an invitation be extended to Alessandra, and with the hesitant consent of his mother, the connecting study was transformed into a cozy, yet elegant, bedchamber for the girl to whom he now pledged his heart.

Holding her a few moments longer, Simon inhaled the jasmine scent that was infused in Alessandra's hair before placing her gently on her own bed. He buried her under the comforter, placed a kiss on her cheek, and quietly whispered, "Sleep peacefully, dearest."

Simon turned at the connecting door and looked back at the young woman who captured him without even trying. *So beautiful,* he thought. *Every inch of her I see is lovely.* Then his dark eyes became even darker, his hands flexed as he remembered the feel of the scars he had touched earlier in the day.

The indescribable torture Alessandra faced every day, married to a beastly devil in disguise, left Simon standing at the door in unyielding petulance.

The marquess pictured her hands, one delicate and the other grotesque. He looked upward at the ceiling, searching for something, he did not know exactly what. A sign? A voice? Anything to help him understand what purpose it served that his beloved Alessandra had to fall prey to the treatment she did.

He flexed his fingers once more as his gaze returned to the angelic faced form that seemed to be sleeping soundly. "Why her, God? If you can hear me, answer me that. Why...her?" Only the sound of silence was the response Simon received.

Chapter Thirty-One

Simon ran. Ran out of the room, through the corridor, and down the steps. The thud of his Hessian boots echoing as his anger grew more intense with every movement. Sweat beaded on his forehead, his hair wild from the run.

As the marquess jumped the last four steps of the staircase, Jasper entered the grand foyer from the red baize door, the duke and duchess from another.

Jasper was the first to address him. "My lord?"

Simon didn't stop his stride when he replied, "Going for a ride!"

"A ride? Simon..." But his mother's words fell upon deaf ears as her son slammed the front door.

Once outside, Simon didn't stop. He kept running, down the front steps and around to the stables where his Arabian steed snorted and bobbed its head as his master entered the stall.

It took no time for the marquess to prep his Arabian. Once saddled, he walked Gabriel out of the stable and trotted him around the grounds before gently hitting his heel against the steed's side. With a slight whinny of acknowledgement, the Arabian took off into a full gallop. He seemed just as restless for a run under the stars as his master. Many a time Simon let Gabriel choose the path they went, and tonight he relinquished that honor to his friend once again.

"Take me away from here, Gabriel! Take me anywhere, but make sure it's away from here."

Simon felt exuberant. He sensed Gabriel shared the same sentiment. Riding at night was something the marquess had not done in a while. The reason he was doing so now began to affect his mood. It was not like him to run from matters and situations. On the contrary, he was of the most adamant nature to confront them.

He pushed the Arabian hard, hoping the sting of the cool, damp air hitting his face would block out the solemnity he sought to forget. The steed obeyed his master and picked up speed. His instinct of where to turn and when to turn was evidence that he had gaited this very path many times before. After a few more twists and turns Gabriel began to slacken his pace. There was a clearing up ahead. A clearing that exposed the edge of Somersby to the local parsonage.

Simon, oblivious to the Arabian's direction until now, pulled Gabriel to a full stop. "You brought me to the vicar?" As if understanding his master's words, the horse snorted. Simon stroked Gabriel's black mane. "Perhaps you're right, my friend. Maybe a chat with someone who has spiritual connections would be able to answer the question that God could not. Then again, likely this *was* the Almighty's answer."

Simon dismounted and held the steed's reign as he walked with trepidation. "Okay, Gabriel. Let us see if we can find some peaceful resolution to help Alessandra. And I suppose some guidance for me as well." The horse responded with a quick bob of his head. Simon chuckled. "You have me at a loss for words, Gabriel. Are you sure you're just a horse?"

As they approached the parsonage, Simon could smell the wood burning inside the fireplace and saw that the side window was illuminated, which meant the vicar was in his study, ready to receive any late night sinners who were too ashamed to be seen by the local villagers in the daylight.

The vicar's son, Andrew, came running outside, told the marquess he could go right in, then took Gabriel by the bit and led him to where the parson's own horse was stabled.

Simon lightly knocked on the door to the vicar's study and entered as he called out, "Vicar Bertram?"

"Ah, Lord Bevan. So nice to see you. I heard that you had been back at Somersby for some time now, but I haven't seen you at any church services."

"Yes, I'm sorry about that, Vicar. I will do my best to be there at the next one."

"Good, good. Everyone can always benefit from attending church, you know."

"Yes, I know, Vicar." Simon stood by the door, afraid to enter any further into the study. The vicar motioned for him to take a seat opposite his own in front of the fireplace. Not sure how to broach the subject of Alessandra, the marquess felt it would only make sense to start with at least mentioning her name.

"Vicar Bertram, do you remember Alessandra Smythson? She's the young girl who used to visit every summer with her parents and brother."

"You mean the young girl who was smitten with you, and at the same time annoyed her brother?" The vicar laughed. "Yes, I remember her quite well. I thought it a shame that she was taken to America when her mother died. She was married off to someone else, was she not? I thought for sure I would be performing a wedding ceremony uniting the two of you. Alas, it was not meant to be. But I hear that she has recently returned to England, and is in fact visiting your family at Somersby."

"She is staying with us for a while, which is why I haven't been to any service, even though I have been home the past few weeks." The parson arched a brow. Simon put his hands up. "Not that I'm using her visit as an excuse for my absence from church."

"Well, why don't you bring Alessandra with you this Sunday?"

The marquess let out a sigh. "Vicar, Alessandra is the reason why I am here."

The vicar remained quiet and held out his hand, signaling Simon to continue. When the marquess did not, but instead fidgeted in his chair, the local church parson leaned forward.

"Is there something troubling you, my son?"

"Actually, Vicar Bertram, there is much that troubles me, but nothing as substantial as what terrorizes Lady Drake."

"Lady Drake?"

"Alessandra. Drake is her married name. One that she should not be using now that her husband is dead."

"Ah, so she is a widow. Poor child. She is too young to be such. Has she any children?"

"No. And this is a good thing. Being a widow is a situation I would not wish upon any young lady. Alessandra, however, is an exception to that very idea."

"Lord Bevan, that is truly an offensive remark to state to a man of the cloth. Why do you seem to fancy the idea that Alessandra deserves to be a widow?"

"I don't necessarily fancy the idea of Alessandra without a husband per se, Vicar. What I fancy is the fact that her husband is no longer alive."

"What is the difference between those two statements?"

"Vicar Bertram, Alessandra was married to a most evil man. He beat her, tortured her, verbally and emotionally abused her. And she is so scarred physically and mentally that she has turned herself into a recluse, to which I am trying to change. Not to mention the fact that she trusts no one, and I mean absolutely no one, not even her own brother. Worst of all, she has herself believing that she has done something so unforgivable that God has put a black mark on her soul."

"How could she believe such a thing as that?"

"I do not know all the details, but she suffers from horrible night terrors. And I think I have given her false hope. I truly believed that I could help her. Help her forget the brutal barbarian to whom she was wed. But I have seen her scars. Her deformity." Simon began to weep. "Oh, God, I don't know if I can do as I promised. To do what I have talked her into asking of me."

Simon looked away, embarrassed by his sobs. Realizing that the vicar would not see it as a sign of weakness, but of compassion, and that there was no shame in crying, the marquess turned his head back towards the one man who could give him some solace. "Alessandra, this once beautiful girl who was such an innocent, who now is permanently maimed, believes in my foolish motto that I am the Warrior and Protector of Heavensford. And it's only because I have coerced her into believing it. I kept telling her to trust me, to listen to me, to believe in me. Vicar, I don't know if I can do what I told her I could do. What I promised her I could do. And what she has come to ask of me."

"And what might that be, my son?"

Simon's voice was anguished. "To save her."

Chapter Thirty-Two

It was well after four in the morning when Simon finally arrived back at Somersby, feeling that the conversation with the vicar had shed a glimmer of hope on his intentions towards Alessandra. It was not impossible he was told, but it would be a difficult journey.

The vicar was informed of everything the marquess had been told, what he saw, and what he felt might have happened during Alessandra's years of marriage. As for the black mark she believed God had put on her soul, neither the parson nor the marquess could understand why she would make such a claim.

Simon quietly climbed the steps to his wing of the ducal manor, stopping before turning down the corridor that led to the connecting chamber of rooms he shared with Alessandra. He touched his hand to the inside pocket of his waistcoat, making sure that what it held, was still there.

He took step after step, praying that what he intended to do in the coming weeks, or even the coming days, would not be detrimental to his cause. To Alessandra's cause.

She asked him to save her. And he vowed to do anything it would take to do just that, even though in his heart, he believed there was only one true and significant way to accomplish the feat he set before himself.

He reached Alessandra's chamber door and touched it lightly, as if his energy would ignite her to wake up and let him in. He listened for any sound and hoped that she did not have any bad dreams while he was gone. He had lost all track of time talking to the vicar and then sped Gabriel on a special errand. An errand that the vicar had agreed would be most beneficial to the journey the marquess had embarked upon.

Was Alessandra's request for Simon to save her the same interpretation that he himself had? Only time would tell.

He continued on down the hallway and once he entered his own chamber, he quietly closed the door. The room was dark but it did not stop Simon from moving with ease around the room. He removed his Hessian boots and stockings. Next he took off his cravat and waistcoat and threw them on a nearby chair. Too tired to care about discarding the rest of his clothing, he laid on his bed, unfastening the line of buttons at the top of his shirt.

Then it touched his nose. The scent of jasmine. *Alessandra.* The marquess turned on his side and there he saw her. The outline of her body curled up in a ball, wrapped in his quilt; the same one he had wrapped around her earlier in the day.

And that's when he knew. Without a doubt he knew that she sought him out for protection. To help drive away the eidolon hauntings that she could not, and to keep them from reappearing when she closes her eyes. Instinctively his gut told him she had a night terror. Why else would she be in his bed, and wrapped in his quilt? And where was he when she needed him the most?

Take me away from here, Gabriel. Those words reverberated in the back of Simon's mind, causing him to curse his own insecurities regarding the one who came to him. A feat he knew must have been difficult. *Trust me.* He clenched his fist and tapped it against his forehead, ashamed that he failed her.

He pulled Alessandra as close as he could, embracing her tightly, and rested his head next to hers. He touched her face tenderly, careful not to wake her from the peaceful slumber she now seemed to have found. "I'm sorry I wasn't here for you when you needed me, sweet one. It won't happen again. After tonight, I swear on my own life, it will not happen again."

Chapter Thirty-Three

Simon had barely closed his tired eyes when the figure sleeping next to him began to move. He waited, not knowing if Alessandra was beginning to have another night terror or if she was only trying to find a more comfortable position. It was not the latter.

A small whimper escaped her lips followed by another twist of her body. Then another whimper. "Stop, Cecil! No more. Please, no more."

Simon bolted off the bed and looked down at Alessandra whose body began to writhe as if in pain. Her hands ferociously lashed out, no doubt trying to fend off the fiend who was attacking her.

Grabbing hold of her wrists so as not to hurt her crippled hand, Simon pulled her to a sitting position. "Alessandra! Wake up!"

"I won't run from you again. I swear. I won't run again."

"Alessandra!" Simon's booming yell echoed off the walls, shocking even himself.

Alessandra opened her eyes and focused on her surroundings. The marquess still held her wrists. "It happened again. The same dream I just had before."

"While I was gone?"

"Why won't it stop?"

Simon tried to pull her close, but Alessandra resisted his embrace.

"I won't hurt you, dearest. I want to help you."

Alessandra began to weep uncontrollably.

"Please, Alessandra. What happened in your dream? Tell me what I cannot see."

Alessandra reached for Simon's outstretched hand. "No, you *can* see. The scars on my back...I was trying to get away from Cecil. He had come home in a drunken stupor. I was in the library reading. When he entered the room, he reeked of not only liquor, but cheap perfume as well. I didn't question his whereabouts because I knew if I did, the response I received would only be one of pain. As it turned out, it mattered not that I remained silent. Cecil flew into a mad rage just the same and said he knew what I was thinking; that he can sense I was questioning him in my mind. He came towards me, but when he tried to grab me he lost his balance and fell. That made his rage even more dangerous. I took advantage of his one moment of clumsiness and ran out of the room.

"When I got to my chambers I locked the door. I didn't know how far behind Cecil was. Apparently he was closer than I thought. Even drunk he could move rather quickly.

"My locked door didn't hold against Cecil and Edwin. Both of them worked together to break it down. I thought I was going to die that night. When they busted through I saw Cecil holding his riding crop. No doubt Edwin kept it at the ready. He took pleasure in delivering pain just as much as Cecil."

Simon didn't speak, hoping Alessandra would continue to tell him the dark secrets she kept to herself. And silently prayed that if she did, her mind would begin to heal itself.

Alessandra's voice quivered. "The sound of that first slice through the air was the loudest thing I've ever heard. And then I heard it again. And again. And again. I don't know how many thrashes I received before blacking out. All

I know is that when I came to, I was lying on the floor, covered in blood. My clothes were ripped to shreds. I later found out that Cecil thought it was his right to have his way with me, whether I was conscious or not."

"He raped you?"

Alessandra turned onto her stomach, away from Simon. "It wasn't the first time. It wasn't the last."

Simon leaned down to murmur in her ear. "You're safe with me, sweet one. Believe my promise." He gently slid his fingers down the back of her nightgown, tracing the crosshatch of scars from the riding crop. Then he tenderly pulled Alessandra back into his arms, cradling her head upon his chest. Her left leg rested against his. He moved his hand in circles on her back, trying to soothe her cries. When he reached for the quilt to cover her, his hand touched her leg, feeling the continuation of welts. The magnitude of her defacement was incomprehensible.

The marquess placed a kiss upon her head. "Try to dream about us. The children we will have. We need to marry first, but we can marry by special license. Maybe elope to Gretna Green. How does that sound? Just you and I, traveling the Scottish countryside for as long as you wish."

When Alessandra didn't respond, Simon continued his soothing tale of what their lives could be like. "It would be magnificent to hear the sound of little feet running through the halls of our very own manor. Would it not, sweet one?" Silence. "Alessandra?" Simon looked down at the young woman he loved. Her eyes were closed. "Good girl. Rest well." Simon closed his own eyes, tightening his hold on her, envisioning himself in her dreams. Envisioning his life with Alessandra.

Chapter Thirty-Four

Somersby Village Chapel, 11 August 1816

"And so sayeth the Lord, rejoice and be glad." The vicar looked out amongst the congregation, skimming the vast faces, and the abundance of those who did not hide their boredom. There were a few who remained attentive, backs straight, and eyes forward. But were they really listening, he silently asked himself. Of course, the duke and duchess were in their usual spot, the first pew on the left. As far back as the vicar could remember, they never sat anywhere else, but that spot. And then he noticed a new face in the back corner, trying not to be noticed. A face he hadn't seen in several years. She must have entered after he and everyone else had come inside.

When the vicar saw the young girl begin to fidget, he quickly turned his head to finish scanning his audience. He brought his hands together to say an ending prayer, and dismissed the congregation. He walked down the aisle towards the front door, almost being knocked over by one little boy who was in such a hurry he didn't see with whom he collided.

"Oliver!" Josie caught her son by the end of his coat sleeve and pulled him back into their pew. "You must wait for the vicar to leave first, Oliver."

"But this was so boring. He said to go and serve God. So I was going."

"Oliver..."

The vicar laughed as he placed a hand on the boy's head. "It's quite alright. I have four boys of my own and they are just as eager to run off as this little lad."

"That is no excuse for my son to not pay attention to where he is going, Vicar. I humbly apologize for his behavior."

"No need. I'm sure he meant no harm, right my boy?"

Oliver looked up at the vicar. Until now he kept his head down expecting a wrath of extreme proportions. "No...no sir." Oliver put his head back down.

"Then all is forgiven. You are just anxious to bask in God's glory outside, correct?"

Oliver, head still down, mumbled his response. "Yes, sir."

"Sometimes I feel like that myself, Oliver. It is a wondrous feeling to be in the midst of God's creation."

Oliver snapped his head up, his frightened eyes once again bright and cheerful. "I like frogs."

The vicar couldn't help himself. He dispensed another laugh, but this one more thunderous then before. "Well now, that's splendid, Oliver! Just splendid."

"But I like them because they scare girls."

"Yes, I know. I was a boy once, too, Oliver."

"Do you still like frogs?"

"I love all of God's creation." The vicar bent down and whispered in the boy's ear. "Now I think I better leave the church so the rest of the people can get home for their midday meal, hmm?"

Oliver whispered back. "Okay."

The vicar finished his journey to the small vestibule and remained there, thanking everyone as they departed for their attendance in God's house on such a beautiful summer day, and bade them all to have a good afternoon.

Saving Alessandra

One person stayed behind. Alessandra sensed him there. Felt his stare. She looked up. In the first pew on the left, gazing at her with his brown eyes was the marquess. She tipped her head forward in acknowledgment. He bowed his head in return.

Alessandra did not move from the corner. Instead Simon went to her. He wanted to take hold of her hands but she was wearing the heavy winter muff he thought was finally discarded.

"Why did you not tell me you wanted to come? You could have ridden with my family."

I wasn't expecting on attending church service, but then I saw your family's carriage leave. Something inside me told me that I should leave as well. I hope I didn't overstep my bounds today when I asked the groom to bring me here in one of your transports? I'll be sure to get your permission in the future should I have need of a carriage."

"You could never overstep any boundaries where Somersby and Heavensford are concerned. Whatever I have is yours to do with as you desire." Simon touched her cheek. "I'm happy to see you out and about. You can only close yourself off from the rest of the world for so long, Alessandra."

"I know. Maybe this is a good place to start."

"Coming to Sunday service and being a part of the congregation is a great place to start." Neither Simon nor Alessandra heard the vicar come back into the church.

"Vicar Bertram, I hope you don't think it rude of me to wait until after everyone else had entered before I took a seat myself?"

"I would have loved to greet you as I did the others, but you will give me that privilege next time, won't you?"

"Of course, Vicar."

"Well now, it is such a pleasure to see you again, my dear. I heard you had come back to England and was hoping to see you. I'm sorry for your loss, my dear."

I'm not. The marquess did not speak the words aloud.

He promised the vicar, during their late night conversation, that he would do his utmost best to refrain from conveying his feelings regarding the succubus that he hoped was burning in hell.

"Grief is a terrible thing, child," the vicar continued. "You can either use it as a positive stepping stone in your life or you can drown yourself in it, missing out on God's world around you."

Alessandra countered, "But what if something happened, something so awful, that it is truly unforgivable?"

The vicar took Alessandra's right hand, the one she did not have to hide, the one that was still perfect, and rested it on his forearm. He then gave it a slight pat before covering it with his own. "Shall we go for a walk, my dear?"

Alessandra nodded, leaving the marquess behind, knowing he would wait for her. Wait for her to bare her soul. And wait for her to forgive herself of whatever sin she so persistently claimed she committed.

Chapter Thirty-Five

"So my dear, how long have you been back home?"

"Since April, Vicar Bertram."

"And how is that brother of yours? He must have been extremely happy to see you?"

"He was. At first."

"Come now, you cannot tell me that the earl was put off by your return to England?"

"Not entirely. I think the reason for my return is what caused the reaction Sebastian gave."

"And what exactly was the reason for your return? Does this have something to do with your statement earlier?"

Alessandra did not answer.

"Do you truly believe that you have done something so wrong, God will not forgive you? He is very merciful, my child."

"I don't deserve His salvation, Vicar."

"And how do you come to that conclusion?"

Alessandra stopped walking. She tried to hide her guilt...her shame.

"Come, sit down." The vicar pointed to a nearby wrought iron bench located in the small garden behind the chapel.

Once seated, Alessandra debated how much she should say regarding her marriage to Cecil. And how much she should confess, believing that the vicar, even though he meant well, would not be able to ease her mental anguish.

"May I ask you a question, my lady?" The vicar shifted his gaze to the covering on Alessandra's left hand.

"You wish to see it."

"If, and only if, you feel comfortable in revealing your hand to me. You need not fear any revulsion from me, child. I have seen much in my fifty years. Brutality towards women is not uncommon, sad to say."

"But why, Vicar Bertram? Why are women, especially young girls, treated this way, as if we are worthless? As if we were born to be beaten, to be mangled, to be broken?"

"I can only say that Satan does his work through many who are receptive to his ways."

Alessandra looked down at the muff covering her hand. Lethargically, she removed it. "I took off my wedding ring in order to play the pianoforte with better agility. This is what I received from my husband in return."

The vicar, shocked at the sight, stifled his voice. He now understood the anger the marquess had been trying to describe to him. It was a few moments before he was able to verbally react.

"Thank you for letting me see your hand. I know it was not easy for you to do so. You may cover it back up if it would make you feel more comfortable."

"It is quite ugly, which is why I wear this cumbersome muff. I don't want to look at it so why should anyone else have to?" Alessandra didn't put her hand back in its heavy covering, but rather used her perfect hand to shield the imperfect one.

"Is this why you feel you are not loved by our Father? As I said earlier, Satan works through those who will abide by his wishes."

"But I *am* evil, Vicar Bertram. It is true that Cecil was

a most devious man, but I, too, have sinned in a most horrific way. In fact, my sin is worse than all of Cecil's put together."

"You must be mistaken, my child."

Alessandra shook her head. "No. I am not mistaken, Vicar. I have done something so terrible that I know God has put a black mark on my soul. I feel it. I live with it."

"Child, God would never do such a thing. Who has put this absurd notion in your head? Pray, do not tell me it was your husband?"

"I know it to be true."

"That is Satan's ranting. You must know that."

"I only know one thing, Vicar Bertram. I am banned from God's grace and will never receive His salvation."

"Perhaps you should tell me what sin you believe you have committed that would keep you from obtaining life with God in heaven."

"It is a most sinful crime. One I have not even told the marquess. He speaks of marriage and children, but I will bring nothing but scandal and pain to the Family Bevan. I have told the marquess to save me, but it will not be possible."

"Jesus is the only savior you need."

"He will not save me for I am not worthy to be saved."

"You are listening to the Antichrist, my child. Listen to what God is telling your heart instead."

"But that is what I mean, Vicar. God has not spoken to me. I have shamed Him. I have lost my place in His kingdom."

"Never! You are a daughter of God. Now stop this blasphemy and tell me why you would rather believe the words of Satan, instead of the words of your heavenly Father!"

Alessandra stood, letting the muff drop to the ground. Her hands went to her belly as she fell on her knees. "The baby."

"What baby, child?"

"Cecil's baby. I fell..." Alessandra hugged herself even tighter. "It wasn't time, but..." She bowed yet further and let out a scream.

The vicar remained in his spot, letting Lady Drake expel her tormented soul, knowing that there had to be more then she was confessing. But he didn't press her to expand on the details. She was troubled enough. Instead, he let silence be his voice.

"He was so tiny. There was no sound...no cry announcing his arrival into the world. When Cecil was told the baby was stillborn, he was so angry with me. A mother protects her children he said."

"Alessandra, you cannot blame yourself."

"I died that day, Vicar. No beating Cecil gave me, before then or after, ever compared to what happened. Nothing ever will."

Overcome with renewed grief, Alessandra tried to stand, but could not. An arm wrapped around her shoulders. She knew who it was without looking.

He told her time and again that she could trust him. That he would help her. That he would be there for her. But would he still be willing if he knew all that was terribly wrong within her?

He claimed to be her warrior. Her protector. She knew he would do anything to prove it. But was she willing to let go of the fear that was keeping her from believing it?

Chapter Thirty-Six

Heavensford, Marquess Country Estate, Berkshire

Simon nestled Alessandra as she lay in his arms, the warmth of his body enveloping hers. He carried her exhausted body up the front steps to the manor, not his parents' ducal estate of Somersby, but his own of Heavensford.

Once inside, Simon quietly dismissed his staff, giving them all a reprieve from their duties until the arrival of Alessandra's maid a fortnight hence. The marquess hoped that this unexpected journey to Heavensford would be the beginning of his new wife's healing.

Ah, his wife. He loved the sound of those words, *his wife*. And this time he made sure it was not a dream.

Resting his head against the pillow, he listened to the embers crackle in the fireplace, and let his thoughts wander over the events that had occurred just that very day.

After seeing Alessandra collapse at Somersby chapel, Simon knew he had to take an adamant stand concerning her emotional catharsis. If he were to be successful in his promise to bring her happiness, to make the past stay in the past, and hopefully forgotten, at least to a certain degree, then he knew he had to ask her. Had to declare the words he had written on paper, the words he scripted in the journals he made for her.

He needed to let her know once again, and without a doubt, that his feelings for her were quite real. That his vow to help her was not made in vain.

He touched Alessandra's face, lightly caressing her cheek with his knuckles, letting her search his eyes for sincerity, for truth, for trust.

The marquess asked, no, he spoke the words. Spoke them with conviction so strong that he almost didn't recognize the deep voice saying them.

"Marry me, Alessandra. Here. Now. Marry me."

"But..."

Simon placed a finger on her lips. "Nay, the only word I want to hear come from your mouth is yes. Yes, you will be my bride."

The marquess felt her fear, saw her fear. "It is me, Alessandra. Remember me? The warrior you grew up with? The slayer of imagined dragons and evil kings? I am still that warrior. But instead of imagined dragons, I am slaying the incubus of anguish that hides deep within your soul. Instead of an evil ruler, I am rebuking the sadist who to this day still paralyzes your waking thoughts and terrorizes your dormancy.

"I am the one with whom you are safe. The one who will create new memories and bring happiness to you. The one who will not deceive you or forsake you. The one who will not hurt you, but love you."

Simon's arms embraced her, afraid that if he loosened his hold, she would run from him. He placed his cheek next to hers. "I am the one you can trust, Alessandra. I am the one whose heart beats for you, and only for you. So I will say my words again for your soul to hear." Simon put his lips against her ear, letting his melodic tone soothe her. "Marry me, sweet one. Marry me."

And she did.

Chapter Thirty-Seven

The ceremony, performed by Vicar Bertram, was brief. His wife and eldest son served as witnesses as the rambunctious voices of the vicar's other children wafted through the open front doors of the chapel.

Alessandra, too exhausted and drained from her emotional confession, let Simon take control. She heard him state he had obtained a special license from the Archbishop of Canterbury and had been carrying it on his person for days, waiting for the best opportune time to present it.

She thought of her brother, Sebastian, but doubted he would be resentful of the haste in which she married.

The marquess did not comment on Alessandra's brother and kept the contents of the last missive he received from his friend to himself. It contained only a few sentences; the last of which read *I hope you can decipher this for I am writing it while quite intoxicated.* Simon used the letter to light a fire that same rainy afternoon.

Concern for following mourning protocol was not voiced by Alessandra as she had done in the past, especially since she knew it would matter not anyway. She was too weak to argue, and with the vicar's support, was convinced by Simon that God would not hold it against her.

She listened to the marquess pledge his love and devotion as he slid his great-grandmother's ring, consisting of a simple emerald stone, onto her right ring finger. When Alessandra stated she had nothing to give him in return, the marquess pulled out the patch of fabric she had embroidered with their initials years before. "I take this as a symbol of your trust in me. My soul was already bound to you when you gave it to me, and I so accept that binding today. This lovely little bit of fabric will be carried upon me each and every day, no matter where I go. I shall cherish it always just as I will always cherish you."

Then Simon kissed her, silencing the vicar before Alessandra would be told to repeat the words usually spoken in a vow ritual by a bride to her groom. One word in particular the marquess wanted to avoid. *Obey.*

Alessandra looked up at her new husband when their lips parted and heard him whisper for her ears only "I love you, sweet one." She couldn't repeat those three words, but saw in his eyes that he understood. That he acknowledged her apprehension and would not hold it against her. And that he forever accepted her for who she was; a young woman who had been broken, physically, emotionally, and spiritually.

Once they said their goodbyes to the vicar and his family, they made a brief stop at the ducal manor to impart their wedding news to the duke and duchess. A trunk was packed with some old dresses for Alessandra that a guest to Somersby had left behind the prior year. When Alessandra refused to take them the duchess explained that the young guest to whom the gowns belonged was no longer in need of them, hence the reason they were left behind in the first place.

"Besides, you two are of similar size, my dear. They will fit you quite nicely. And it will be lovely to see you rid of those dreadful mourning gowns."

Alessandra caught her husband's priggish grin when

she conceded her mourning wardrobe to the duchess.

"Please make sure they are burned to unrecognizable ashes, Mother, will you? And burn this monstrosity as well." Simon held up the heavy furry muff that had been attached to Alessandra for months.

"Simon!" Alessandra tried to grab it from his hand but he held it high out of her reach.

"My lovely wife, you will be fitted with more beautiful attire as soon as it can be arranged. For now, these used gowns will suffice, along with your personal items, which do not include this rodent."

"I need that, Simon."

"You do not need this, Alessandra. I have given you a more subtle hand covering, which if I may elaborate, is much less noticeable. Please let me rid you of this, sweet one."

Alessandra knew he was right. But the muff had become a part of who she was. It was a necessity to keep others from being shocked by her hand's lack of normalcy. To keep questions from being asked.

She looked at Simon and saw his concern. If he was to help her break loose from the chains that held her captive to the past, then she needed to help him to help her. Alessandra was reluctant to let the marquess destroy the one thing she could depend on, but after a short hesitation, she conceded.

The matter of her clothes settled, the couple joined the duke and duchess for a simple repast of chicken with fruit compote. A round of tearful hugs ensued before the couple left for Heavensford where their lives as husband and wife would begin.

It was arranged for Josie and her son to join them at a later date. The marquess also sent word to Oakes in London that he was to travel to the country estate as well. Alessandra was skeptical at first, but Simon reassured her that for the next two weeks, their maid and valet would not be needed.

And so, here they now were, lying on the marquess' bed; the marquess watching his wife rest peacefully in his arms. Tonight, all was as it should be.

Chapter Thirty-Eight

Alessandra watched her husband as he lay in a deep slumber, moonlight framing his body. She did not wake when they arrived at Heavensford, nor did she wake when he placed her on his bed and removed her gown and slippers. But that was all the undressing he did of her. Even his own clothes he did not shed.

She was still dressed in her chemise when she awoke some time later and was relieved to find that Simon did not have his way with her. She knew he would not. Honorable men do not take advantage of the ones they love, she thought. And the marquess was a very honorable man.

How long would he not pressure her to consummate their marriage? She knew it would have to happen sooner or later. Simon was at an age where talk of an heir would be a prominent subject in their conversations. She was sure of it. But would she be able to give herself in such a carefree manner? He's already seen her tangible scars, but the emotional ones were just as execrable, if not more so.

Alessandra contemplated what she understood to be her wifely duties. And being married to a marquess turned those duties into undeniable obligations.

She watched as the last embers in the fireplace extinguished themselves out, leaving behind a chill in the room. Alessandra shivered slightly, almost wishing she had stayed in the warm bed.

Subtle moonbeams coming through the window were the only light source, yet it was bright enough to find her way around her husband's chambers. Not seeing her own trunk, she searched Simon's massive wardrobe and found a gentleman's dressing robe. She was surprised by its simplicity. The fabric was not made of expensive silk and there was not one stitch of extravagant embroidery that she could see. In fact, the more her eyes adjusted to the room's darkness, the more she saw that even her new husband's furnishings were just as simplistic.

Alessandra paused at the edge of the bed to look at Simon once more before leaving the room to explore its endless spaces. But once she peered out the chamber door and saw nothing but darkness, she changed her mind.

"You're not running away from me already, are you wife?" Simon asked teasingly.

Alessandra jumped. "Simon! I thought you were sleeping."

"Nay, sweet one. As soon as you left my side my peaceful repose ended."

"Why didn't you say something then?"

"Because I wanted to watch you watching me."

"But your eyes were closed."

"Not completely. And I must say I was very disappointed that you found my robe. I rather like you covered in only moonlight."

Simon couldn't see her face, but he was sure it held a bit of color.

"The fire went out and I was chilled. And I am wearing a chemise so I wasn't covered in only moonlight."

"Ah, but a very thin chemise."

"Simon!"

"Have I embarrassed you? I didn't mean to, sweet one, but I apologize just the same." Simon held up the edge of the quilt. "Come back to bed. There is still an hour or two before the sun begins to rise."

"I'm...I'm not tired."

"Indeed? I don't think I'm tired anymore either. I feel quite rested, in fact."

"But you want me to come to bed."

"We can just talk, Alessandra. Nothing will happen that you do not wish to happen." Still not able to see her face clearly, Simon began to leave the bed.

"What are you doing?"

"I do not like having a conversation with someone I cannot see, so I am coming to you since you do not want to come to me."

Alessandra took a step back. The door blocked her from going any farther.

"Are you frightened, Alessandra? Why are you afraid of me?" Simon reached her side.

"I...I..."

The marquess took hold of her hands and placed a kiss on each one. "You are safe here, Alessandra. I will not force myself upon you if that is why you want to leave this room."

"I am scared, Simon. I don't know..."

Simon reached around her to open the door. "Come. We will go elsewhere. The kitchen, perhaps? I will make us some tea. How does that sound?"

"You are angry with me, are you not?"

"Of course not. Why on earth would you think such a silly thing as that?" Simon took her by the hand and led his wife from the room.

"Because we did not...because I did not..."

Simon stopped and took hold of Alessandra by the shoulders. "I want to say something to you and I want you to always remember it. I am your husband. I am also a marquess who is first in line for my father's dukedom. And as such not only do I have a healthy appetite and want to ravish you, but I also need an heir."

"Which has me feeling guilty because..."

"No, Alessandra. Do not feel guilty. Let me finish what I want to say. What you must remember. I will never try to bed you unless you come to me first and request me to do so. Do you understand?"

"But..."

"I love you. I want to father your children. I know in my heart you will be a great mother. I want nothing more than Heavensford to be filled with the pitter patter of little feet running through the halls. But at the same time I want you to not be afraid of me."

"My experience..."

"I know, my love. You do not need to say anything. There was no gentleness in your first marriage. Not an ounce of tenderness did Cecil show you. He took what he wanted when he wanted it and how he wanted it. You have made that very clear. And that is why I am letting you have control. You will tell me when. I am in no hurry. And I certainly am not going anywhere."

Simon resumed his path towards the kitchen, Alessandra still in his grasp.

"Simon, wait!"

He stopped. "What is it, my love?"

"There is something I want to ask you. Something I could not bring myself to ask in front of Vicar Bertram."

"About the baby who died? He was stillborn, Alessandra. You are not to blame. If Cecil would not have been chasing you in a drunken rage, you would not have been running. Please do not keep upsetting yourself."

"It's not that. If I become with child, and it is stillborn, what would happen?"

"Then we would try again."

"And again?"

"As many times as we could, sweet one."

"But what if I have become barren as a punishment from God for what I did?"

"Stop thinking foolishly. God would never do such a thing."

"But..."

Simon placed a finger on her lips. "Then we will accept whatever God has planned for us."

"You answer so simply, yet with great faith. I am not so sure I can do the same."

"You are still grieving the loss of a child. But in time you will, Alessandra. All you need is time."

Chapter Thirty-Nine

Alessandra looked lovely and youthful in the pale yellow gown that the duchess had packed for her. Tiny white daisies were embroidered along the hem as well as the edges of the cap sleeves. She wanted to pin her hair up, but Simon convinced her to leave it down.

"There is no need to bother with such fuss, sweet one. It is only I in your company and I prefer your hair to be down. It's quite beautiful. You're beautiful."

"You flatter me, my lord. Is there pretense behind your compliments?"

"You think I would lie? I would never do such a thing, Alessandra. Do you not believe me when I say you are beautiful?"

"I did once, but that was a very long time ago."

"But now that I am your husband, you think I tell a falsehood. You wound me, sweet one."

"Don't be angry with me. It is difficult for me to accept such flattery as truth, let alone listen to you speak it."

"My dear wife, your days will be filled with me speaking nothing *but* truths. I suggest you forget whatever nonsense the other fellow filled your head with and replace his cruel words with my honorable ones."

"You think you are honorable? Let me see. You

dragged me to your estate without my maid, gave the servants the next two weeks off..." Alessandra put her hands up before continuing. "I know they work hard and deserve it, but that means I have to eat what you cook. And so far it has been nothing but toast, fruit, and whatever is biting in the lake. I do not think that qualifies as cooking, sir."

Simon placed a hand over his heart. "My dear, you wound me again. Have you no shame?"

"None. I can speak truth just as you speak truth."

"Ah, my wife is truly a little minx. I like it." Simon wiggled his brows.

To his surprise Alessandra laughed. And it was the most glorious sound he had ever heard inside the walls of Heavensford.

Chapter Forty

Alessandra stared at the emerald ring on her right hand. It was simple, yet exquisite; even more so when the sunlight danced upon it. She pulled it off her finger, setting it on the pianoforte.

Sheet music was already laid out, as if calling upon the marchioness to play, beckoning her, regardless of her inability to use both hands to create a melody with the simplest of chords.

Alessandra looked once again at her ring, trying to block out her late husband's voice that was taunting her from his grave.

Stupid girl. Stupid, stupid girl! It's your own fault you cannot play. I've told you time and again to never take your wedding ring off.

"Ah, here you are, my sweet."

Alessandra, startled by Simon's arrival, grabbed the emerald ring and tried to put it back on her finger, but to no avail. Her attenuated fingers were too weak to hold it steady and so it fell, rolling across the floor, and landing by her husband's feet.

The marquess bent down to pick it up. As he did so, he glanced at his wife who moved to stand on the other side of the pianoforte, farther away from him.

"Are you alright, sweet one? Don't fret, I have your ring."

"I'm so...sorry. I didn't mean to take it off."

Simon stepped towards his wife, but the closer he got, the more she trembled.

"Dearest, what's wrong?"

"I...I need to go."

"Need to go where?"

"I don't want to be here."

Simon furrowed his brows. Concerned for his wife, the marquess took a step back. "I just want to put the ring back on your finger, my sweet. Nothing more."

"I didn't mean to drop it. It won't happen again."

"It's quite alright, Alessandra." Simon stepped forward again, but this time his wife took a step back. "Come here, my sweet, don't be frightened."

The marchioness covered her ears with her hands, trying desperately to not hear her dead husband's menacing laugh.

"Stop! Stop laughing at me!"

"Alessandra, I am not laughing." Simon tried once again to get closer to his wife, but she cowered to the floor.

"Leave me!"

You deserve a beating for dropping the ring, you stupid girl!

"No, it was an accident. I didn't mean to drop it!"

"Of course you didn't mean to drop it."

Stupid girl. Your new husband is going to whip you, just like I whipped you. Or maybe he'll break your other hand as I should have done.

"No! Go away!"

I shan't go away. I will never go away, you stupid girl.

"Oh, God, make him stop. Tell him to stop!"

"Alessandra, what do you want me to stop doing?"

"Him. It's him. I can hear him."

"Hear who?"

"Cecil."

"Cecil is dead, Alessandra."

"He's here."

Your new husband cannot help you, you stupid girl.

"Alessandra, look at me." Simon ran to his wife, knelt before her, and tried to pull her hands away from her ears. "Look at me!"

Her eyes shifted to look at Simon.

"Listen to me. Listen only to me, Alessandra."

She didn't respond.

"When you were married to Cecil, what happened in the music room?" Alessandra shook her head. "You need to tell me, dearest, so I can help you." Again she shook her head.

He will not get rid of me, you stupid girl. You are mine, not his.

"No, I am not yours!"

"You *are* mine, sweet one. As I am yours."

"Cecil. He controls me. He won't stop talking."

"Give me your hands, Alessandra. Give them to me!"

She moved them from her ears and held them out to Simon. He reached out, pulled her body into his, rested his head on top of hers, and began to rock her in his arms. "Everything will be alright, sweet one. Do you hear me? Everything will be alright."

"I'm scared. He seems so real."

"It's okay. He can't hurt you anymore, my love. He's dead. Always remember that. He's dead."

Simon kept his wife cradled in his arms, soothing her with his words, and silently prayed that what he just witnessed would not happen again. But he knew that Alessandra's emotional scars ran much deeper than he anticipated. The journey his wife faced, in seeking freedom from the sadist who still ruled her from his grave, was going to be a very long and difficult one.

Chapter Forty-One

Simon put away the emerald ring he had given Alessandra for safe keeping. Not just to protect the ring, but also to deter any future parallels between her past and present. Not knowing how to calm her, the marquess gave her some laudanum, just enough to relax her. He stood by the edge of the bed, arms crossed, and watched her listlessly submit to what he hoped would be an untroubled afternoon doze in the arms of Morpheus. He didn't know how long she would remain asleep, so he had to act as quickly as possible.

The marquess knew she brought her journals with her, not just the ones he gave her at Somersby, but several others he never saw before. Perhaps in those he would find some answers. Some indication of what he was facing.

He quietly, yet efficiently, searched her trunks for the journals. He was not proud of himself. He knew he should have asked her permission to read them, but if his wife wasn't strong enough to discuss all the horrid events of her marriage, especially the maiming of her hand, then Simon decided he would have to rely on his own devices to find the answers to his questions. He wanted to help, but he also wanted to keep her on a safe path that would not result in any repercussions like the one that had transpired earlier in the day.

The wedding ring...why the ring? he kept asking himself. He did not care that she dropped it. It was an accident. He also did not care that she had taken it off to play the pianoforte. But he knew who would. *Cecil.*

The marquess thought back to the music room. Alessandra practically jumped off the bench, trying desperately to put the ring back on her finger. She was frightened that she was caught not wearing it. *Her left hand. The pianoforte. She closed the fallboard. The ring. Her broken left hand. The fallboard.* Simon's pulse raced. His fury began to build. *That's how you did it, isn't it? You bloody spawn of Satan!* He was determined more than ever to find his wife's journals.

The first trunk held nothing other than her personal effects; undergarments, nightgowns, jewelry cases, and jasmine oil. He lingered longer than necessary, enraptured by the jasmine scent. It had become his ultimate form of intoxication. His thoughts went immediately to his wife and the difficulty he had with abstaining his desire to have her. Every hold, every nearness, every slumber was a battle he fought constantly and one that was getting harder to control.

Simon carefully eased the lid back to its closing position and quickly looked at his wife. She had not awakened. The marquess began a search of the second trunk, ruffling through a few remaining lightweight gowns his mother had packed for Alessandra, and another small pile of undergarments. He wondered how many chemises a lady actually needed. Lastly, lying at the bottom of the trunk, he found a gossamer gown of pale lavender.

The marquess recognized it at first glance. He pulled it from the heap, skimming the ornate embroidered rose design of white and gold silk threads with his fingertips. Suddenly, the memory of him and Alessandra dancing at the last ball he attended before leaving the country came to life. Only at the time, he didn't know it was to be their last meeting. Neither did Alessandra.

He remembered their waltz, the scandalous dance he taught her during the secret meeting he arranged in the inner garden. If it wasn't for the rules of propriety set forth by the *ton*, Simon would have been able to waltz with her for all to see. As it was, her age had dictated less risqué promenades around the ballroom. And no more than one dance per gentleman. Simon gritted his teeth. He wished he would have gone against propriety back then; for if he did, he was certain her life would be much different now.

He refolded the gown and placed it back at the bottom of the trunk, followed by all the other pieces of clothing he had usurped. He stood, looking for the third trunk. He could have sworn he had seen three trunks belonging to Alessandra be placed on their carriage. It was not as big as the other two, so it was small enough to hide inside a piece of large furniture. He faced the wardrobe and took a step towards it.

"It's not in there."

Simon quickly turned on his heel. "Ah, you're awake, sweet one."

"Yes, and what you seek is not in this room."

"So I gather."

"Tell me, dear husband, what exactly do you hope to find in the third trunk?" Alessandra unraveled herself from the coverings Simon layered upon her. She paced her words to enunciate her displeasure. "The contents...are most personal...and not to be...looked upon...by anyone."

"Forgive me. I only meant to seek knowledge of how your hand became..."

"Contorted. Fractured. Grotesque. Shall I go on?"

"No. You announce those words as if you think I believe your hand identifies you. I do not. It does not."

"You told me to trust you, my lord. Yet as I slumber you rummage through my belongings as if I were a thief stealing away your most precious valuables."

"I do not think that, Alessandra. And please do not use proper titles when addressing me. You are not my servant."

"Then what, pray tell, shall I call you? Liar? Untrustworthy? There are many names I can use, my lord. Choose one and I shall be more than happy to oblige."

"Do not call me any name other than Simon. If you cannot bare to have my name cross your lips, then so be it. But do not ever call me...my...lord."

"As you wish." Alessandra hesitated before giving a deep curtsy, infuriating the marquess.

"You are purposely provoking me, my love. If it's a ruse to make me forget about the third trunk, it will not work. I will search this house from top to bottom, every inch of it, until I find what I am seeking."

"You have no right to touch my personal possessions. They are mine and mine alone!"

"You forget, dearest, that you married a marquess. Whatever is inside the walls of Heavensford belongs to me. Therefore, your personal possessions are rightfully mine!"

"You will force me to relinquish them to you?" Alessandra tugged on the chamber door, then turned back to view her husband. "Fine. Search for the third trunk if you wish. But take heed, Simon Thane Bevan, Most Honorable Marquess, you will be opening Pandora's Box. Whatever consequences may come of it will be on your shoulders to bear. That, I promise you."

Simon stood still. He did not move as he watched his wife leave the room. *Pandora's Box? Consequences?* If she thought to deter him from searching for the third trunk containing her journals, she was mistaken. Her words only seemed to have proliferated his interest and desire to find the books post haste.

He heard the front door slam, and suddenly realized he had lost whatever ground he had gained in his relationship with his wife. And to his own shock, he thought he heard Cecil laughing from his grave.

Chapter Forty-Two

"How dare he say that he owns my possessions," the marchioness grumbled as she ran down the stone steps. "You do not, my lord. Nor do you own me." She cupped her right hand over the left, trying to calm her seething ire. She turned, facing the front of the manor. "Do you hear me, husband? You do not own me!"

Alessandra looked up at one of the windows and caught a glimpse of his outline moving away. "I see you, Simon. Do not even attempt to hide from me. If you want to watch my every move, then stand your place like a soldier instead of a coward."

His form did not come forth.

"You call yourself a warrior? A protector? You are neither, my lord."

Still, the marquess did not return to the window.

"I know you can hear me, Lord Bevan. I began to trust you. To believe in you." Alessandra took a few steps back, searching all the windows, but still the marquess was nowhere. Her heart palpitating, she searched the first window once more. No form. No outline. No Simon.

The sound of hooves coming around the side of the manor house made Alessandra even more furious. "That perplexing man is going riding?" She ran to where the dirt path led from the stable to the front grounds. And there she saw him, her husband, The Honorable Marquess of Heavensford, sitting atop his Arabian, Gabriel.

Alessandra looked up at her husband.

Simon looked down at her. He arched a brow.

"How dare you think to go for a ride when you have me in such a state!" Right hand on her waist and left foot tapping, the marchioness blew on a curl that had come loose, partially blocking the vision in one eye.

"How dare I, you ask? Surely you jest, my dear wife? You are the one who left the argument in the first place. Not I."

"I had to leave."

Simon arched his other brow.

"You mock me with your facial expression?"

"I challenge you to explain why you needed to leave."

"Because you instigated the situation, my lord. You..."

Simon held up his hand. "Before you continue, please remember that I have already told you on one occasion to never call me my lord."

"You, husband, are incorrigible."

"Pray tell, dearest, how am I beastly? I have never lifted one finger to your person. I have never played with your mind. I have never, and I mean never, toyed with your heart. So excuse me if I do not agree with your accusation. Perhaps you meant to call me incorruptible? On that, I will agree."

"Do you realize that what you did today was something a person of honorable character would not have done?"

"I only did what I did because I need answers, Alessandra. I cannot keep abiding by your wishes. Yes, you have told me some details, but not all. We are married now, and as such, we should be honest about everything. It is the only way I know of that will help me to help you."

Alessandra looked away, a slight breeze blowing more curls loose from the pins that were holding her hair back from her face.

Simon let out a sigh. "I know what I did was wrong. But what happened in the music room scared me. You have never reacted to anything while awake. At least not to the extent that you did today. Had I known that the music room and the pianoforte were, for lack of a better word, instrumental in what happened to your hand, I would have sealed that ill-fated room off."

Gabriel snorted, his body becoming restless.

"Give me your hand."

"Why?"

"I want you to come with me, Alessandra."

"Where are you going?"

"Gabriel needs a good run. He has not been through the fields in a couple of days."

"I don't want to go."

"Dearest, come with me."

"No."

Simon clenched his jaw. "So be it. I will not beg. I will be gone a few hours as I will be making a stop at the lake before returning."

"What need do you have to stop at the lake and at this time of day? The sun will be setting soon."

"Because sweet one, you have me in such a whirlwind of frustration, both emotionally and physically, that I need to jump into that lake to cool off before I explode!"

"Oh." And with that small response, Alessandra smacked Gabriel on his hind quarter, sending the Arabian off in full frenzy. "Sorry, Gabriel, but that infuriating master of yours made me do it."

The marchioness watched as the Arabian picked up speed, but her smirk of delight was short-lived when Gabriel suddenly made a sharp turn at the end of the drive. Alessandra froze. "He's coming back?" She tried to move, but her legs ignored her plea to run. Shaking her head, Alessandra kept her eyes on Simon as he headed straight back to the spot where her powerless body now stood.

Chapter Forty-Three

Simon managed to grip the reigns just as Alessandra smacked his horse. "Why, that little minx." His equestrian skills quite excellent, if not exceptional, gave the marquess the advantage needed to control the Arabian's unexpected bolt. "My wife will be the end of my sanity, Gabriel. Mark my words, you are fortunate to be a horse."

The marquess let Gabriel gallop to within a few feet of the pathway's end, then he steered the Arabian into a complete turnaround. "Come on, my friend. It seems my wife likes surprises. Let's not disappoint her."

The horse snorted.

"I agree with you, Gabriel. It would be rather rude to leave the lady behind."

Simon barely touched the heel of his boot against the Arabian's flank, sending the horse into a full gallop back towards Alessandra, who seemed to be shaking her head.

"Hah, the minx is surprised but good, my friend. In fact, she looks to be a bit shocked."

It was only a matter of a few short moments before the marquess reached his wife.

"Give me your hand, dearest. I have decided that I should not have all the fun."

Alessandra didn't move, nor did she try. In fact, to her

own regret, and to Simon's, she was utterly speechless.

"You did not expect me to come back after that little stunt you just pulled?"

Alessandra took a step back, but Simon took one forward on Gabriel, and kept advancing with each step back his wife took.

"I can do this all night, my love. But it will be much easier if you just relinquished yourself to my request and accompany me to the lake."

Simon watched his wife's eyes shift from him, to Gabriel, back to him, then ever so slowly turn her head to look at the stairs behind her. When she glanced back at Simon, he had already jumped down from the Arabian's back.

"You may run if you wish, my love. But like it or not, you will be going to the lake."

Simon let the marchioness reach the top step before he went after her. He heard her shriek as she quickly shut the front door. Not a shriek of fear, really, but one full of...laughter? The marquess looked back at his horse, standing where his master left him. "Gabriel, do you hear our lady? She's laughing." The Arabian, always comprehensive of his master's words as though he were a human reincarnate, bobbed his head.

The marquess placed his ear against the door, listening to the echoing sounds of his wife's giggling and taunting inside.

"That's it, sweet one. It's about time you realize that you have the power to create new memories. Taunt me, my love...control me. Whatever you want of me, I will do. Help me to help you, sweet one."

Gabriel, inpatient for a run, snorted.

"Sorry, friend. My ride will have to wait." Simon left the front veranda and quickly disposed the Arabian of its saddle. "But you will not miss out. Go run." The marquess patted Gabriel's hind quarter, sending him on a solitary journey of Heavensford.

Simon looked up at the windows. He grinned. "My love, you cannot hide from me. Show yourself."

Her shadow materialized at the same window the marquess himself had been spying through earlier. The difference, however, was that his wife had opened the sash. Her voice reached Simon's ears.

"Is that a challenge, husband?"

"Would you like it to be?"

"If you cannot find me in a quarter hour, what is my prize?"

"Anything your heart desires. But what, pray tell, is the prize for me should I find you, wife?"

"A kiss."

"Just one kiss? Come now, you can tempt me to seek you with a better prize than that."

"Oh, very well, two kisses then."

"And?"

"And?"

"And. I am a future duke after all. I deserve a more substantial prize."

"And...whatever *your* heart desires."

"My heart desires for you to be happy, sweet one. Nothing more, nothing less. Just...be happy."

"Then I'm afraid your prize will only be two kisses. But you have to find me first."

Simon's voice rippled. "Oh, I will find you sweet one. I will find you. And you *will* be happy."

Chapter Forty-Four

Alessandra looked for a place to hide. "So, you think to best me at this game, my husband? It is I who will do the besting." The marchioness went from room to room until she covered both wings. "Come on, think Alessandra. There has to be a good hiding place somewhere." She frantically tapped a pointer finger against her lips, trying to jolt her brain into thinking of a spot. *The inner garden.*

She ran down the back staircase the servants use and stopped in her tracks at the green baize door. She was no longer alone.

The marquess called out to Alessandra from the front foyer.

She did not respond.

Simon called out again, this time both his voice and his boots echoing closer.

Drat!

Her husband entered the kitchen.

Be still, Alessandra.

Silence.

Just keep still.

It seemed an eternity before hessian boots were heard retreating back through the kitchen entrance.

Then it happened. Unexpectedly. Loudly. She sneezed.

Double drat!

The sound of hessian boots, however, did not return.

He's waiting for me to come out.

Heart pounding, Alessandra lightly pushed on the green baize door, that until that moment, was her only shield. She inched her head out to take a peek of the kitchen, silently thanking the staff for maintaining noiseless hinges. When she felt it safe to leave her hiding place, she closed the servant's door behind her.

The marchioness kept watch of the red baize door that led from the kitchen out to the foyer as she tipped toed towards the back door. Her hand no sooner touched its handle when she heard her husband on the back stairs. *No!*

She quickly changed course and ran the other way, going through the red baize door she had been watching. Hessian boots followed suit.

Alessandra couldn't help herself. Too full of anxiety, good anxiety, she looked back over her shoulder at her husband and squealed. "Not fair, Simon. You did not give me a quarter hour in which to find a place to hide."

"You are absolutely right, sweet one. I actually gave you a full half hour."

The marchioness didn't stop her pace. She ran out the front door, down the steps, and headed towards the garden, hoping to arrive at its center core before her husband reached her.

She took one more look over her shoulder and saw him. Her husband, Simon Thane Bevan, Marquess of Heavensford, standing on the front veranda, and he was laughing. Not a menacing laugh but a very robust hearty laugh. And it was contagious.

"There is no need to continue to look for a place to hide, my love."

Alessandra chortled in response. "To the inner garden is where I am going. If you can catch me before I reach the archway..."

"Are you giving me another challenge?"

The marchioness didn't answer, but kept on running. She passed by Gabriel who unbeknownst to her, had gone for a quick run and returned to his master while she was inside the manor house trying to hide.

"Detain your master, Gabriel, and I will give you as many apples as you wish to eat."

The Arabian bobbed his head, making Alessandra laugh even harder. "Good boy, Gabriel."

Once the marchioness reached the garden fountain, she turned, looking for her husband. He was not behind her. Winded from all the running she had done, she stopped.

She reached her hands into the cool water, allowing herself to rest a moment before continuing her quest to the inner garden. Both her hands looked distorted as she swirled them just below the surface. The sameness shocked her, for she knew they would never be the same again.

Not wanting to see the actual disfigurement of her left extremity, Alessandra looked away when she pulled her hands out of the water. She patted her face with her right, keeping the left one down at her side. She had resigned herself long ago to the fact that there was nothing that could be done to change her hand's mangled appearance.

Alessandra heard Simon's whistling approach, but she did not continue her path. Instead, she waited for her husband. Waited for him to comfort her, as she had grown quite fond of his strong embraces. Waited for him to once again do what had been an impossible feat for many years. Until this day, when he helped her to forget about herself, forget where she had been, and forget about what she had physically become, even if it were for only a short while. But most of all, she waited for her husband because deep down inside, she realized she truly loved him.

Chapter Forty-Five

Alessandra tried to push the curls out of her eyes, but they only remained defiant, cascading freely as if they held a life of their own. Knowing she must look a mess from running, she pulled out the few pins left dangling in her hair.

She bent her head forward, combing through her long dark tresses with her right hand, hoping to gain some sort of composure. And that's when he reached her. The tips of his Hessian boots came into view below the fringes of her curls.

Alessandra felt the warmth of Simon's hand remove hers from the tangled mess she was creating. She looked up, his hand conveniently behind her head, holding onto her massive mane.

No words were spoken. They didn't need to be. She slightly tipped her head, acknowledging that she knew he wanted to kiss her. That he wanted to claim his prize. But she also knew that he would not attempt to kiss her unless she was ready for him to do so. And that was her dilemma. She wanted, but was not ready.

"You are hesitant, sweet one. I can see it in your eyes."

"I made a promise and I will not renege on that promise."

The marquess let go of Alessandra's hair, allowing it to

fall freely down her back. He took hold of her left hand, kissed each finger softly, then gently held it against his chest.

"My heart belongs to you. *I* belong to you. Forever and always. No matter what."

Alessandra took hold of Simon's left hand, and placed it against her bosom. "My heart is beating quite rapidly."

"As is mine, my love."

"I want to say these words that are jumping about in my head, but yet...I'm honestly frightened of them. Speaking of love is so easy for you."

"Your smile is enough for me, sweet one. And the sound of your laughter. That, in itself, sang to my heart today."

"Life was so easy when we were younger, remember?"

"It will be again." Simon leaned forward, still holding his wife's enfeebled hand, and placed a small kiss on her forehead. He stepped back, just enough to look down into her eyes.

The marchioness placed her right hand on Simon's shoulder. She tilted her head up, biting her lower lip.

"I believe, dear husband, that I owe you a kiss."

"I am willing to forgo the prize promised me on one condition."

"What condition?"

"I want you to promise me that you will never back down from me. If I do something that truly angers you, then yell, scream, throw a tantrum; if the mood strikes you, then throw an object at my head if you wish. I don't care what you do, but do not be afraid to confront me. I will not hurt you, ever, Alessandra. Do you understand what I am saying to you, sweet one? I want you to fight back."

"But what if I am too scared to fight back? Or don't want to do anything except be alone?"

"Then tell me that very thing and I will walk away."

"And if I lock myself in a room?"

"No locks. If the door is closed I will know not to enter. I pray you never want to shut me out, sweet one. But if you feel the need to do so, for whatever reason, I will not, and I mean I will never, ever, force my way into your sanctuary."

"Truly?"

"Truly, dearest."

Alessandra stood on tip toe and kissed her husband's cheek, his stubble rough against her lips. She edged her mouth to meet the corner of his and gave another kiss. "Thank you." She kissed him again, this time fully.

Simon leaned into her, but cautiously, wanting his wife to control the level of their contact.

A light breeze blew, entwining her jasmine scent with his sandalwood, surrounding them both with aphrodisiacal redolence. It was then that Alessandra broke their embrace, yet leaving her less than perfect hand in his.

Simon pulled gently on a long curl that blew across his wife's face. He stepped closer, twirling the ringlet around his finger. "What would you like to do now, my love?" Simon held onto the curl.

"Just be here. In the garden." Alessandra closed her eyes for a brief moment, reminiscing of a time from long ago. "No, the inner garden is where I was going earlier. That is where I want to be now. With you."

Simon, still holding his wife's hand, led her from the fountain towards the archway of the inner garden. That, he thought, was where he wanted to be, too. The peaceful paradise that was just as important to him as it was to her.

For in that small haven of blooming rose variations, honeysuckle, jasmine, and other exotic nature, was a memory of the time when he taught Alessandra to dance the waltz. The time when he first kissed her. A time when neither one knew what evil existed in the world.

The marquess would create bliss for his wife once again. Only this time, there was no need for him to let her go.

Chapter Forty-Six

Alessandra set herself at Simon's desk in the library. Quill in hand, already dipped in ink, her journal waiting for her to write, but the words did not come. She stared at the feather as she stroked it across her perfect hand, remembering her husband's light caresses from days before.

Overwhelmed, and also confused by the sensations foreign to her body, Alessandra abandoned her fear of what she was used to experiencing. Once in the inner garden, all thoughts of the past eight years escaped her, and in their place, were the gentle touches of a new husband who shattered the invisible gate surrounding her heart. Never, she thought, would the wall she built up to protect herself be broken down. And yet, through Simon's understanding of who she had become, passion, laughter, and even some happiness, had begun to remove the chains that held her shackled to what was. A new beginning was declared that day. And when all was said and done, Alessandra had lay in her husband's arms and cried.

The marchioness, resolving to keep recent bedding events to memory only, closed the journal and laid the quill to its side. She removed herself to the oversize leather chair next to the window, where the orange streaks of the setting sun stretched behind the trees lining the gardens. Leaning back, legs curled under her, she closed her heavy-laden eyes, immediately falling into a reminiscing repose.

Honestly, she recalled saying to her parents, *so what if a man has his hand on a girl's waist and that they are close to each other. It's just a dance and one that would be watched by everyone in attendance. I beg you to change your minds and give me permission to dance the waltz.*

The next thing she remembered was her brother, Sebastian, leading her out to the inner garden of Heavensford, where upon arriving at the archway, Simon was waiting for her. He uncrossed his arms, took Alessandra by the hand, told Sebastian to stand guard for possible gossipmongers, and guided her through the opening.

She had never been to this part of the garden before. In fact, she never knew it existed until then. It was a private sanctuary consisting of various blooming rose bushes, an abundance of honeysuckle, several patches of jasmine, and so on. Alessandra did a complete turn, her senses mesmerized by the surroundings. She faced Simon, knowing he was watching her reaction to the beauty and hypnotic aroma that was the inner garden.

"So, Alessandra, I hear you were displeased with the decision of the *ton,* as well as with your parents, regarding your request to dance the waltz."

Still in awe of the nature around her, she gathered enough thoughts to respond. "Indeed, I was very displeased. Would it have been so terrible? I mean, our families have known each other for many years. We are friends after all, are we not? Surely two friends dancing the waltz is not as scandalous as two strangers dancing the waltz."

"Maybe not, but propriety dictates that there is an age requirement for such."

"Oh, poppycock."

"Why Lady Smythson, you have shocked my ears."

"I do not believe that ridiculous statement at all, my lord. I am most confident that you have heard language much worse when among your rakish friends, my brother included."

"Truly you do not think I am a rake, do you? My heart would be seriously offended."

"Hmm...I don't believe that comment either, my lord. I doubt I could be held in such high regard as to cause damage to your pride."

"But I do hold you in high regard, Lady Smythson." Simon stepped closer. "Which is why I am going to teach you to waltz."

"But you yourself just said propriety..."

"I only stated what propriety dictates. I did not say I believe in its rules, especially when it keeps me from dancing with a most endearing friend."

"Is that all you will ever see me as, Simon Thane Bevan? A friend? Nothing more?"

"I *did* call you endearing, Alessandra Willow Smythson. Do you not like me to think of you as endearing?" When she didn't answer, Simon chuckled. "Come now, it is a rather affectionate term. Perhaps you would like a different one. What would you say if I called you adorable? Or cute?"

Alessandra scrunched up her nose. "Cute? Cute is for children. I am not a child."

"Of course you're not. I never said you were." Simon took her right hand and placed it in his left, gently putting his own right hand just below her shoulder blade. "We are wasting time with our banter. We can talk afterwards." He instructed her to rest her left hand on his upper arm. "That's it. Now just follow my lead. And do not look down at your feet."

The marquess began to hum, trying to glide Alessandra amongst the greenery. After a few missteps, she began to catch on to the rhythm of the dance. He held her closer than was proper decorum, but he didn't care.

Neither did she.

As they completed a full turn about the exotic foliage, the need to speak overwhelmed Simon unexpectedly. Caught off guard by an unanticipated desire to voice his growing affection for his childhood friend, who up until recently was only thought of as his best friend's younger sister, the marquess stopped abruptly, forcing Alessandra to lose her balance, which in turn caused Simon to tighten his hold upon her.

Alessandra looked up at the marquess and furrowed her brows. Confused by the intensity in which Simon was looking back at her, she checked her stance. "I'm sorry, did I misstep again?"

Simon did not loosen his hold; rather he tightened it even more. "This inner garden never contained jasmine. I instructed the gardener to transplant some from another estate. Do you know why Lady Smythson?"

Alessandra shook her head.

Simon leaned into her ear and lowered his voice to a whisper. "Because your scent is jasmine. When I am restless during the night I come out here, and in one bewitching moment, I'm reminded of you."

Alessandra moved her gaze away from Simon, trying to focus on the tree behind him.

"Ah, I have rendered you speechless. Not an easy feat. Then I shall continue while I can. There is another reason I had Sebastian bring you out to the garden."

"What reason?"

"I am going away for a while."

"When? For how long?"

"At least a year. I will be traveling with my cousin, Quin."

"The Duke of Veston?"

"He has not been the same since his wife passed away. He needs me."

Alessandra stepped back and cursed herself for not having a handkerchief to dab her eyes. "Forgive me, I don't know why I am reacting so."

"Is it because you have fond affection for me?" Simon wriggled his brows, but Alessandra was not amused at his attempt to humor her. "Oh, dearest, a year is not very long at all. It will go by quickly, I assure you." Simon tipped her chin up. "Just think, when I come back, maybe the *ton* will have changed its views on the proper age for a young lady to waltz."

"How can you joke when you will be leaving?"

"Because it is who I am and how I handle uncomfortable situations."

"Please don't go, Simon."

"But I must, dearest. I am needed elsewhere for a while."

"I will truly miss you, Simon Thane Bevan."

"And I you, sweet one."

A movement at the archway caught their attention. Sebastian whistled like a robin, not very convincingly, but it still served its purpose as a pre-conceived warning to alert Simon when someone was coming.

"You best get back to the house, Alessandra, before people begin to wonder where you have gone off to. And with whom."

"I'm not worried. You set Sebastian as my cover."

"Yes, well, just the same, you should leave now. I will follow in a few minutes."

Lady Smythson reluctantly began to walk away. She felt a tug of her hand and turned around.

"Wait, Alessandra. I want you to know that I think you look beautiful tonight. In fact, the most beautiful I have ever seen you."

"Thank you." Alessandra felt heat rising to her cheeks. She bowed her head.

"Nay, don't hide your sweet face from me."

"I believe you have made me blush, Lord Bevan. It's unladylike to let a man see how he affects her."

"I think it's quite lovely to see you this way."

And before he let go of her hand he kissed her. A

subtle, simple kiss to let her know he indeed held her in high regard.

Chapter Forty-Seven

Simon watched Alessandra from the door of his study. He had been in the stables talking with his groom who returned to Heavensford. The rest of the servants were due back the following morning.

Seeing his wife frown, the marquess stood ready to wake her if she became restless. Her night terrors had subsided much over the past few days; still, a lone tear rolled down her cheek. Simon didn't budge from where he stood. Instead, he waited in quiet observance.

Alessandra rolled her head to the side, blinking her eyes. Sandalwood permeated her nostrils. She rolled her head again, focusing from where the scent was coming.

"How long have you been watching me take a nap?"

"Only briefly, but long enough to see a tear glisten your cheek."

Alessandra touched her face. "Oh."

Simon knelt before her. "Was it *him* again?"

"No. This time I dreamt of you."

"What happened that I made you upset as you slumbered?"

Alessandra sat up and cupped her right hand against her husband's cheek. "You left me."

"When?"

"It's irrelevant. We are together now."

"No, when did I leave you? Surely, it was of some importance if my departure affected you as you slept."

"Please don't think of it. It was a long time ago and need not be mentioned. Besides, my dream was actually quite a happy one."

"Until the end it seems. Please tell me about it."

"You are a most stubborn man."

"But you love me anyway." Simon wriggled his brows.

"You did that very thing in my dream."

"What, move my brows?"

"I was dreaming of the time you taught me to waltz."

"Ah, yes, the dance that gave the upper matrons all an apoplexy."

"Only because they were too old and jealous of the enjoyment the younger set derived from it."

"You begged to dance it, sweet one. And I saved the day, did I not? You would not have learned it if not for me."

Alessandra's face grew solemn.

"Oh, dearest. What is it?" Simon pulled Alessandra onto his lap and leaned against the overstuffed chair.

"That's the same night you told me you were leaving for a year with your cousin."

"A thorn in my side when I think about it, my love."

"I left for America before you returned."

"I know, Alessandra." Simon kissed the top of his wife's head before resting his chin upon it. "I'm sorry."

So that's why she was crying. Had it not been for his one year journey with the Duke of Veston, he would have been present to help her through the grief when her mother suddenly passed away. And, most importantly, he would have stood before her, refusing her father to take her to America.

Simon realized that many events transpired which had played a hand in Alessandra's removal from her home. Further contemplation resulted in anger at himself, proving he thought, that he was no better than Sebastian, and no less guilty. Upon his return to England, Simon was met with the news that Alessandra's father had embarked on a journey of his own the day prior, taking his daughter with him.

One day. She missed my return by just one day.

The marquess blew on a raven-colored curl, redirecting it from continuing its tickle of his nose. He tightened his arms around his wife. *At least she's dreaming of me now.*

Chapter Forty-Eight

The Coach and Four hit a rut in the road, almost sending Sebastian off his seat. He regained his balance, but let Alessandra's missive regarding her marriage to Simon fall to the floor. Another missive, one from his late father's solicitor in America, was hidden away, carefully placed in the inside pocket of his brown tailcoat.

The letter did not hold much detail regarding his sister's marriage to Cecil, but it did answer the question concerning the details of the fiend's demise. Apparently, the deviant's sadistic cravings were known throughout the lower class circles. But those less fortunate were not the only victims. Sebastian groaned, knowing his selfishness was the beginning of Alessandra's road to tortuous debauchery. He clenched a fist before slamming it against the inside wall of the carriage. "I almost killed her!"

The sound of scratching wood jolted Sebastian to look up. "M'lord, is everything alright?"

"Just get me to Heavensford as quickly as you can, driver."

"Aye, m'lord." The driver slid the board back into place, shutting himself off from further contact with the earl.

How Alessandra's dead husband fooled their father, a man of high intelligence and common sense, Sebastian could not fathom; other than that their dear father was not the same man after the passing of their mother. Before her death, the family patriarch calculated risks cautiously and could sniff out a blackguard of ill will a mile away. There was nothing Sebastian could do about the past, except reside himself to the theory that Cecil played upon his father's delicate state of mind. And Alessandra's as well.

Sebastian looked down at the missive that lay near his booted foot. He retrieved the piece of parchment, scrolling over its contents once again. He concentrated not on the meaning of the words themselves, but rather the lack of graceful penmanship which scripted them.

He crumpled the letter into a ball, squeezing as hard as he could. Remembering Alessandra's difficulty holding a quill forced Sebastian to grit his teeth. His lips were instantly parched and thirsty. The earl's fingers twitched. He flexed them, trying in vain to ease the desire to reach under his seat; to avoid the craving of seeking out the bottle of brandy he stashed in the secret compartment; to crush the ravenous addiction and need he had for the amber liquid and its flow of fire down his throat.

He believed his stock at Smythson house to be depleted. That is, until his butler came upon the last and final bottle. Sebastian had intended to instruct the servant to rid it from the house, but the command was never voiced. Instead, he hid it himself, thinking that the only way to conquer his dependency was to gain will power against it.

His strategy had seemed to be working the past fortnight. And *was* working still this morning. Until he found himself seated in a box, for hours on end, briefly stopping once to rest the horses and to obtain a bite to eat. His timeless closure allowed him the perusal of Alessandra's missive over and over again, pressuring the earl into a reflection of his own guilt and self-pity, causing Sebastian to consider surrendering to the infernal liquid.

His nerves a wreck, he became more distraught with

each passing minute. His day started off happily enough. After all, he was traveling to visit his newly married sister, the wife of his best friend. What was more exciting news than an amiable match to someone whom the earl trusted with his own life?

Without a drink to hold, Sebastian's extremity didn't know what to do. The twitch worsened.

Blasted!

He rubbed his face, feeling the rough stubble that had grown since that morning. He licked his parched lips. The brandy called out to him.

"Get a hold of yourself, Sebastian. Liquor is not the answer."

The carriage hit another rut in the road; this time the earl did fall, his body doing a complete rollover, landing with his back towards the front of the carriage, which made his foot hit the secret compartment under the seat he fell from, which unfastened the spring door, which, therefore, released the bottle of brandy. Sebastian watched as it rolled towards his hand.

"Ah, bugger."

Chapter Forty-Nine

Heavensford, Marquess Country Estate, Berkshire, 12 September 1816

The manor was all a buzz with preparation for its visitors. The marchioness, who had neither organized nor attended a social gathering in eight years, reluctantly agreed to a small country fete with only the closest of family in attendance. A larger London affair had been decided upon for the following Season.

"Besides, my love, propriety dictates that a ball must commence to officially announce our union. It is my duty to introduce the new Marchioness of Heavensford, you know."

"You are a very vexing man, dear husband."

"You love me more when I'm in such a mood."

"Hmm," was all she said before turning her attention back to her penmanship tablet.

It had become a daily routine of late, scripting the alphabet with Oliver. Already exhibiting intelligence beyond his six years, the boy theorized that if Lady Bevan couldn't write properly with her left hand, than perhaps she should learn to use the other. A simple solution, indeed, but one that was painstakingly difficult to master.

Another pastime added was embroidery. When the marchioness confessed to her husband that she longed to feel the softness of silken threads, he surprised her with a basket full of them. An array of vibrant colors, as well as softer tones, met her eye.

"Oh, they're lovely. Thank you."

Simon kissed her and then walked away, leaving Alessandra to create. She was embracing life as she had done years before, albeit, one small step at a time, but nevertheless, each one of those steps was a triumph.

And now they were about to receive visitors to their home. Not many, but knowing his wife was breaking away from the recluse she had been, made Simon feel ever the more victorious. It was not an easy journey, but one that became less intimidating, emotionally and spiritually, with each passing day.

Physically, Alessandra's hand was forever altered. This is the only part of her that would not see change. The fear Simon had was the level of discomfort the marchioness would experience with the passing of time. He sent several missives to various renowned physicians, unbeknownst to Alessandra, inquiring into deterioration of damaged bones. Not one reply received held a positive prognosis. In fact, they were all quite dismal, explaining that such injury could never be anything but excruciating as time wore on.

Only one item remained left to be settled, and that was the sound of little feet running through the halls. Children were a difficult subject to discuss with Alessandra and one that Simon treaded with great care. Even though they had consummated their marriage weeks before, their intimate relations since had been few.

Grief for a child lost is always a great inner struggle the vicar had stated. But the traumatic incident that triggered the loss was making Alessandra's grieving process that more debilitating. Time would be the healer according to the clergyman. Time. And a lot of prayer.

The marquess and marchioness waited at the bottom

of the veranda steps as a Coach and Four rolled to a stop.

"Are you excited, my love?"

"Extremely."

Simon looked at his wife. "This will be good, I'm sure of it." He grasped Alessandra's hand, silently praying that everything would be more than just good.

A footman unlatched the carriage door, but no one descended the steps. A pungent smell, unfortunately, did. It was a combination of the most acrid odors.

Simon took a step towards the carriage and stopped in mid stride of the second, only to find himself pulling forcefully at his cravat, cursing its intricate knot. He signaled Alessandra to back up and a servant to look inside the Coach and Four. If there was a dead body in there, which the vile aroma suggested, the marquess did not want to be the one to discover it. A low mumbling was heard, confirming that the occupant of the carriage was indeed alive.

Holding his cravat securely so that it covered his nose and mouth, Simon stepped up to the door and looked in. Masking himself was a waste of time. His nostrils were immediately flooded with the stale smell of someone in a drunken stupor. And was that vomit?

The marquess swiftly turned around, taking a few steps before deeply inhaling non-putrid air, grabbed his wife's hand, and pounded up the steps into the house, slamming the front door behind them.

Chapter Fifty

"No one lets Lord Ashleigh in this house until he cleans himself."

"Simon, you cannot be serious?"

The marquess raised a brow. "You think I jest? Did you not smell the man?"

"Then where do you expect him to bathe if he is not permitted to enter without first being clean? And significantly odorless."

"Well, my love, since your brother wishes to behave like a horse's arse, then he can bathe where they reside. In the stables."

"That is a very humiliating thing to do to a man, Simon, especially an earl who happens to be your best friend."

"You believe his actions do not warrant such treatment? Where was his respect towards *you* today? Or to himself? His arrival was an embarrassment. He was invited to our home and he shows up not only completely foxed, but covered in his own vomit. No, sweet one, brother or not, earl or not," Simon ran a hand through his hair before continuing, "best friend or not, he deserves to be treated with nothing more *than* humiliation."

"Simon, please..."

"The matter is closed, Alessandra. Sebastian is lucky I don't make him clean the inside of that carriage. *My* Coach and Four, if you please. As it is the seats will have to be reupholstered, and the floor will possibly need to be replaced since I am quite certain that it may be ruined as well."

"Is the damage truly that bad?"

"Well, my love, it seems your beloved brother got bored once he finished off his liquor. To keep himself amused he carved my family crest into one of the planks. It would have been fine if he were an artist and did a superb rendition; however, he is not, and so neither is the rendition."

"I'm sorry."

"For what? You are not responsible for your brother or his asinine stupidity."

"I know, but I'm still sorry."

The Marquess touched his wife's cheek. "Me too, sweet one."

An hour later Sebastian was impeccably clean, meticulously shaven, and remarkably odor free. As for his state of mind, well, there were only so many miracles that Simon could expect his friend's valet to perform in one day.

He instructed the servant to put his brother-in-law to bed and to leave him there. "Do not wake him for dinner. Let him sleep off his malady."

"Yes, Lord Heavensford."

"If the earl should happen to wake, which I will be surprised if he does, then bring him a plate of food. Under no circumstances is he to leave his chambers without my permission."

Simon noticed the valet's overly quiet demeanor, which was so unlike the servant's character.

"I seem a harsh man to you, do I not, Brooks?"

"Never, sir."

"I can be a kind spirit, you know. That is, when no one

antagonizes me to act differently."

"Yes, Lord Heavensford."

The marquess regarded the valet's graying hair and sad eyes. They were not so sad the last time he had seen the man. Simon pondered a moment, but he could not remember ever seeing Sebastian's valet any way other than affable.

"Tell me, how often have you found Lord Ashleigh in his cups?"

The servant's eyes became wet, yet not one tear spilled forth. He fought the urge to cry, which gave Simon proof that something was terribly wrong.

"You can trust me, Brooks. Whatever you say to me will remain in my confidence. I give you my word."

The valet's shoulders slumped suddenly, as if he aged twenty years. "I'm sorry, my lord. I am grateful Lord Ashleigh has a friend who cares. I care, too. Immensely. I have been in the Smythson household for many a year, as you know, and I have always thought of the earl as the son I never had."

The marquess motioned for the valet to sit, afraid the old man would fall over from the shakes that abruptly manifested. Or were they always there? The man was aging quickly before Simon's eyes.

"To answer your question, my lord, I'm afraid it has been more than I wanted; although, the past two weeks my master seemed to have come about and didn't touch a drop." The valet's voice began to crack, releasing the tears he tried so diligently to keep from falling. "But today..."

The valet couldn't continue. He stared down at his hands that lay listless in his lap. And sobbed.

Simon acknowledged the sight as that of a broken man weeping for a son who was defeated by a force beyond his control. Guilt was a powerful opponent. And that battle, the marquess knew only too well, began when Alessandra returned home to England.

Chapter Fifty-One

Simon read the time on the mantel clock. Exactly two in the morning. The chimes didn't sound. Or maybe they did and he didn't notice. It didn't matter anyway he thought. He was too engrossed in the letter that lay before him on his desk. A letter that Sebastian's valet was directed to deliver to the marquess, if his brother-in-law had not yet retired. He had not, so it was.

After perusing the note, Brooks was given the marquess' consent to bring Sebastian to the study, after which the valet was ordered to go to bed. Before he departed the room, he was further commanded to forgo his duties the next day. He started to refuse Simon's offer, but the old man was too tired from the day's events to keep up the argument. He thanked the marquess several times as he closed the door behind him.

"That gentle soul is worried about you, Sebastian."

"I know."

"You know? That's all you can say?"

"What else do you expect me to say?"

"How about you're ashamed of yourself for what happened? Or how about you tell Brooks you're sorry because he had to clean the regurgitated liquor off your body? Or Brooks, I'm sorry I have been nothing more than a half-witted arse. Not to mention the apology you owe me for the damage you so unselfishly placed upon my Coach and Four."

"Fine. I will apologize to him tomorrow. Is that better?"

"Don't give me an attitude, Sebastian. I know your head must be in the process of splitting itself into infinite pieces, but if anyone deserves to be condescending, it's your valet."

"I know."

"Again with I know. What the devil is the matter with you? He's a valet, a servant, someone of no importance according to the *ton*, but he is still a human being with feelings."

Sebastian leaned his head back against the leather chair in which he sat. "Scold me for saying this, but...I know."

"He has no family so he thinks of you as his son. He has coddled you ever since you were a little boy, and all you have done lately is put him through misery. Not to mention upsetting your sister today. I won't even begin to tell you how I feel about that."

"You don't have to. I know."

The marquess rolled his eyes. "This is not a game I'm playing with you, my friend. Not here. Not now. In case you have forgotten, I have been feeling just as guilty and responsible as you for what has happened to Alessandra."

"Really? Explain it to me then. Because as I see it, if I would not have been such an arse eight years ago, my sister would not have been taken to America, would not have been married off to that, that...demon of darkness, and would not have endured the torture she has. So tell me, *my friend*, how is your guilt the same as mine?"

"Do you not remember I left for a year? Had I been here..."

"Had you been here you would have done what, Simon? Married her? She was only sixteen. Pray, do not tell me your little flirtation the last night you saw her

Saving Alessandra

before your journey was a serious one?"

"It could have turned into a very proper and accepted courtship had I stayed."

"You know that is not true."

"You think your parents would have turned down my request? Our families were old friends. I agree, Alessandra was a bit young, but I'm sure I could have still spoken for her."

Sebastian rubbed his face. "Look, I am not saying you didn't care for her then, and I am not going to waste any more time arguing the point. We both love her. I think we can agree on that much."

"I love her dearly. If I didn't I wouldn't have married her."

"Are you saying that to convince me you love her? Or are you trying to convince yourself that being shackled to her wasn't done out of guilt."

"I should throttle you for that remark."

"Good. It wasn't out of guilt. Just checking."

Not much more was said in reference to Sebastian's drinking itself, except that they both concluded he needed to refrain from doing so, for his own health, and for Alessandra's peace of mind; and for poor Brooks.

The letter from Sebastian's solicitor in America, however, evoked a different opinion altogether. But while the earl had lay in unconsciousness earlier in the day, Simon swore off drinking whenever Sebastian was in his presence; and therefore, the subject of pouring himself a snifter of brandy at the present moment, and offering one to the earl, was out of the question. Also, the marquess had Oakes hide all the liquor.

In its place, Simon had to settle for a different kind of amber liquid. Tea. It had been setting on his desk since before Sebastian had first entered. He poured himself a cup, hoping it would quench his thirst. It wet his throat, but it didn't calm his frazzled nerves that seemed to have become tremendously agitated with Sebastian's first *I know.*

Upon reading the solicitor's note for what seemed the thousandth time, Simon looked up at the earl and exhaled an expletive. One his tongue has never spilled, but it was one he believed summed up not only the severity of the entire situation, but the personal rage he fought so valiantly to mask.

An awkward moment of silence befell the gentlemen, sparking each one to eye the other. Until the unexpected crash just outside the study, and a little boy's voice when Simon yanked open the door.

Oliver, on his knees, his hands frantically reaching for the tiny, colored glass balls that were rolling across the floor in every direction, looked up. "I'm sorry, Lord Bevan. I dropped my marbles."

Chapter Fifty-Two

"Oliver, why are you up at this hour? And why are you playing with marbles? You should be sound asleep."

"I wasn't playing with the marbles, my lord. I dropped them."

Simon, already flustered from one conversation, silently counted to ten before starting a new one.

"Oliver, why are you not in bed?"

"I came to show you something, Lord Bevan."

"You wanted to show me your marbles?"

"No, my lord."

"What then?"

Oliver motioned with his pointer finger for Simon to bend down. He did.

"What is it, lad?" Simon stretched his own lengthy arm and snatched up the last marble that wandered aimlessly away from Oliver when the boy tried to pick it up.

"A secret."

"A secret?"

"Yes, my lord. But you mustn't tell my mother or Lady Bevan."

"That depends, Oliver."

"Please, my lord. I won't be able to show you what I want to show you unless you promise not to tell."

Simon placed his hands on Oliver's shoulders. "Is it a secret of something you did that you weren't supposed to do? Did you break something and it needs to be fixed?"

"No, sir."

"Is it something that will hurt their feelings?"

"I don't know."

"Will they get angry if they find out your secret?"

"I don't know."

Simon heard Sebastian snicker. Growing weary for his bed, the marquess relented.

"I promise."

"Cross your heart, hope to die, stick a needle in your eye?"

Sebastian's snicker turned into a low belly rumble, which stopped as soon as Simon turned his head. The earl put a finger to his lips, but not before he let out a snort.

Simon glared.

"Sorry."

The marquess returned his attention to Oliver.

"I don't like the needle in the eye bit, but I promise I will not say a word about anything you show me."

Oliver placed his nose against Simon's, staring him in the eyes without blinking.

"Okay. I believe I can trust you. But what about..." Oliver pointed towards Sebastian.

Simon arched a brow. "That's a good question. He does look a might untrusting, doesn't he?"

"Now wait a minute." Sebastian began to rise from his seat.

"Keep still, Sebastian. I was only teasing."

"Lord Bevan?" The boy's eyes, just moments before full of excitement from finding the marquess awake in his study, suddenly looked empty. Broken.

Like Brooks. Simon pulled Oliver into his arms and hugged him. "It's alright, lad. Whatever you wish to show me, or tell me, will not be mentioned to anyone else."

Sebastian cleared his throat, resulting in a glance from Simon, who inclined his head in the earl's direction.

"But Lord Ashleigh needs to know, lad. He can keep a secret." The marquess drew an imaginary X over his heart. "My word of honor."

Oliver handed his secret box to Simon to hold and walked over to Sebastian, who had already knelt down, arms out to receive him.

"I promise, Oliver." Sebastian looked into the boy's eyes. "You have my word of honor, as well."

Oliver turned so that he was facing both men. He glanced towards the door, saw the marquess had shut it, and took his secret box back from Simon, only to set it down on the seat Sebastian had vacated. He raised the lid.

"I don't hear Lady Bevan cry anymore. She is always smiling now. Does she no longer dream about the bad man and his bad friend?"

"Do *you* dream about the bad man and his bad friend, lad?" Simon asked.

"All the time. I think it's because of my box."

"What's in your box, Oliver?"

The boy lowered his head and pulled out a folded piece of parchment. "Evil."

Chapter Fifty-Three

The marquess and Sebastian sat on the floor, Oliver across from them, the secret box in the middle of their circle. They studied Oliver, closely watching him as he meticulously unfolded the piece of paper, then refolded it. His knuckles turned white as he held it tightly.

"What is that, lad?" Simon was the first of the two men to interrupt the room's uncomfortable silence.

"A drawing."

Simon hastily scanned the contents of the box. "Are all those pieces of paper drawings?"

Oliver nodded.

Sebastian asked the next question. "Are they drawings you did? Drawings of things you saw happen to Lady Bevan?"

"I heard things, too, my lord."

Simon reached out and slid the parchment from Oliver's fingers. He opened it. Reluctantly and hesitantly, but he opened it. He passed it to Sebastian, whose hand immediately became unsteady upon viewing the picture.

"Give me the next one, lad."

The next was worse than the first. And so on it went. Drawing after drawing. Until there were only two pieces of paper left in the secret box.

"This one is of me, Lord Bevan."

"Is this a picture of when the bad man told you to find a switch?"

"No, Lord Bevan."

Simon carefully opened the paper. A streak of red was falling from a hand. A simple picture, yet powerful beyond words. The two men, enraged that an innocent boy had seen and heard what he did, were stunned further.

"Did the bad man cut you, lad?" Sebastian's voice had become shaky.

"Yes, Lord Ashleigh."

Simon spoke in nothing more than a raspy whisper. "Let me see your hand."

Oliver turned over his tiny hand, exposing a two inch scar that ran diagonally across his palm.

Simon took hold of the boy and pulled him into his lap. "I'm sorry." He kissed Oliver's head, embracing him strongly as he began to rock back and forth. "I'm sorry."

Oliver held onto the marquess, his own sobs mixing in with those of the man who had become an instant friend upon their first meeting.

"I don't want to have scary dreams of the bad man anymore, Lord Bevan."

"You won't lad. You won't. I'll make sure of it. I promise."

Sebastian did not wait for Oliver to give the last drawing. The earl retrieved it from the box himself. The sketch needed no explanation. The riding crop in the air, a woman with long black hair lying on the floor, red lines across her back, a man with horns and a tail stood next to the woman, while another man laughed. It was this last picture that sent the Earl of Ashleigh's emotions over the edge. He left the study then, ran out the front door, down the veranda steps, and fell onto his knees, wailing convulsively.

Simon stayed behind, rocking Oliver; his hold on the boy grew even tighter.

"You're a brave little boy, Oliver."

"I thought she died, my lord. She stopped crying. But I didn't come out of my hiding spot. Lady Drake, I mean Lady Bevan, told me not to leave it no matter what."

"It's alright, lad. You did what Lady Bevan wanted you to do. If the bad man would have seen you, he would have hurt you, too. Lady Bevan didn't want that to happen."

"But I should have gone for my mother when I didn't hear any more noises."

Simon loosened his hold. "Look at me, Oliver. You were scared. I would have been scared, too. You did a brave thing by obeying Lady Bevan and staying in your hiding spot."

Oliver rubbed his eyes. "The bad man always called Lady Bevan a stupid girl. He yelled at her all the time. If he didn't like her why did he marry her?"

"I don't know, Oliver."

"She never went out, especially after he broke her hand."

Simon jerked his body away from Oliver, moving the boy off of his lap.

"Did you see the bad man break Lady Bevan's hand?"

Oliver did not answer.

"It happened in the music room didn't it?"

Again, the boy did not respond. Simon watched him fight like a brave foot soldier not to cry. The battle was a short one.

"Come here." Simon pulled Oliver back onto his lap. "Shh. It's alright, Oliver. Close your eyes now. Everything will be alright."

The marquess closed his own, listening to Oliver sob, while the rest of the house was awakened by Sebastian's cries on the front lawn of Heavensford.

Simon stood, Oliver in his arms. Then he saw her. Standing in the doorway, not looking at him cradling Oliver, but at the crude drawings scattered upon the floor.

Chapter Fifty-Four

"Why didn't you tell me Oliver had heard your beatings, and in some cases, seen them? Not to mention he suffers from night terrors about the bad man and his bad friend, just as you had."

"I was afraid if you knew you would question him. I didn't want that to happen. I did what I thought was best for him."

"Alessandra, the look in his eyes when he even mentions your dead husband is enough to make my skin crawl. And did you know that monster cut him?"

"Oliver said he fell on a piece of broken glass, but I sensed it was Cecil's doing."

"Did you confront the barbarian about it?"

"No."

"No? Why not?"

"Do not turn what happened to Oliver onto me, Simon. It would have been a huge mistake had I gone to Cecil. My questions would have only provoked him to beat the boy again."

"Again? Ah yes, the switch. Oliver briefly mentioned a switch, but that was weeks ago at Somersby."

"Cecil only beat him once that I know of. And then the cut on his hand. If he was hit more than that I have no knowledge of it. We never found bruises on him other than that one time. We tried to always keep an eye on him and have him hide when Cecil was around."

"It matters not, anyway, now does it? The damage has been done." Simon flexed his fists. "I can still feel Oliver's trembling body in my arms. I will never forget it. Just like I will never forget the first time I held you."

"Oh, Simon." Alessandra ran to her husband's side.

"Oliver needs a father figure, Alessandra."

"He has a mother who loves him."

"But he needs a man in his life. Someone who will be able to make him feel protected, secure. Which begs the question...where *is* his father?"

"He died, or so I was told. When Cecil hired Josie, there was no husband. Only she and Oliver."

"I don't want the lad being afraid, Alessandra." Simon looked down at his desk, the pictures from the night before still visible. "I'm going to burn these. There's no need to keep them."

The marchioness touched her fingers lightly to the one of Oliver's hand. "A mother should protect her children," she said in a hushed tone.

"What did you say?"

"Nothing."

Simon gathered the drawings together. "I suppose you wrote about these events in your journals?"

Silence.

"It's alright. You don't have to answer me. I know you did." The marquess put his hand up at Alessandra's gasp. "No, I did not go looking for your journals. I've kept my promise."

"I think it's best to leave them hidden."

"Or burn them."

"Burn them?"

"You wish to keep those as mementos? Are your scars not reminders enough?"

"There are thousands upon thousands of words I have

written. Perhaps one day..."

"They will serve a purpose?"

"Yes."

"What purpose exactly?"

"They may explain..."

"Wait...I wanted to read them to gain insight into everything that has happened to you, yet you stated you hide them from me because they are personal. But now you say they may be used to explain what has happened?"

"Simon..."

"No, help me to understand why, as your husband, I am not allowed to peruse them if what I have been trying to gain all along is nothing *but* an explanation to every incident, every burn, every cut, and every scar?"

Alessandra stood still. And silent.

"There's something else, isn't there? Something you're afraid to tell me."

A knock sounded on the door. "Enter," Simon called out, but his eyes remained on his wife.

"I'm sorry for interrupting, Lady Bevan."

"No need to apologize, Josie. Lord Bevan and I have finished our conversation."

Josie, not much older than the marchioness, was of a smaller frame, with lighter hair and complexion. Seldom did she make her presence known in the house, unless it was of a necessitous nature. In fact, the only times Simon recalled ever seeing the maid was on her walks with Alessandra and Oliver, but rarely anything more than that.

Simon looked from Alessandra to Josie, to the rolled parchment the maid held in her hand, then back to Alessandra.

"Has a missive come for me, Josie?"

"No, Lord Bevan. 'Tis for my mistress."

Alessandra shook her head, and silently mouthed what Simon thought was *no*.

"It is time, Lady Bevan."

"Not yet, Josie."

"Please, Lady Bevan, do not think me rude, but it is indeed time."

"Time for what?" Simon asked.

"Nothing."

"Alessandra, my dear wife, this is the second time within the past quarter hour that you told me something was nothing."

Josie stepped forward and laid the rolled parchment on Simon's desk. She glanced briefly at the marquess while retracing her steps to the door. Before closing it she met the eyes of her mistress. "We made a pact, my lady. It is time."

Chapter Fifty-Five

Simon waited for the door to click. "What did your maid mean by that?"

"When she said it is time?"

The marquess gave a slight bow of the head.

"The parchment. It is a document. And one of great importance. I believe it will shed some light, or it may raise more questions. Regardless, this is one piece of parchment I will not let you burn."

Simon carefully unrolled the paper. Alessandra watched as his eyes scanned the document, once, twice, then back and forth a third time.

The marquess looked at his wife. "This is real?"

"Yes."

"Does Sebastian know about this?"

"No one knows. Except Josie and myself. And now you."

"The journals..."

"Explain the details of all that happened. And why I chose to do what I had done. But that document. That precious piece of paper would have been my death sentence had Cecil found it. This is who I am, yet who I could not be."

"Oliver's mother."

Alessandra tried to hold back the tears that now found a path down her cheeks. "He is mine, but he must *not* know."

"There's no threat anymore, sweet one. To you or to the boy."

"It will confuse him. He's much too young to learn the truth of his heritage right now."

"He has a right to know, Alessandra. So does Sebastian. Your brother needs to know he has an heir."

"I will tell Sebastian, just as you will tell your parents. But Oliver..."

"The longer you hide the fact that you're his real mother, the more resentment he will feel when you finally tell him the truth."

"He won't understand. Besides, I fear that finding out Cecil was his father will be too devastating for him. Do you not agree?"

"Why does he need to know that he is Cecil's son? What have you and Josie told him thus far?"

"Lies, obviously. Oliver believes his father was a foot soldier who was killed in battle."

"And he and his mother just so happened to have journeyed to America for what reason?"

"To find family after Oliver was born."

"And?"

"Must your inquiry continue?"

"Sweet one, that boy has been through a traumatic experience, just as you were. The sooner he knows you are his real mother, and why you kept his identity hidden, the better. He is a very intelligent boy. He deserves to know the truth."

"I don't want Oliver to know that his father was the *bad man*."

"My father was the bad man?"

Simon and Alessandra turned towards the door.

"Oliver!" they both exclaimed in unison.

"I don't want the bad man to be my father."

Simon came around from behind his desk. "Come here, lad."

Oliver did not move from the doorway.

"Oliver, listen to me. He's not your father. Not anymore."

"But he was."

"And now I am."

Oliver looked at Alessandra. "Did you not want to be my mother?"

"Oh, Oliver. Of course, I did. You have to believe me dearest when I say I wanted you to know. But your father was such an evil man. In order to keep you safe I couldn't let the bad man know you were his son, which meant I couldn't let you know I was your mother. Who you were had to be kept secret."

Simon tugged Alessandra's hand, pulling her to sit on the floor with him. He motioned for Oliver to join them. The boy scuffed one foot, then the other, repeating the action until he made his way into the room.

"I know it will be difficult for you to understand everything, lad, but I promise you that when you are older you will. Lady Bevan, your mother, wrote journals that we will keep and give to you when we feel you are old enough to read them. For now, I want you to try to forget about the bad man. He is gone. Forever."

"But Josie is my mother."

"No, Oliver. I only helped to keep you safe. Your true mother is the one sitting before you." The maid entered the study, kneeling down next to Oliver. "I will always love you, Oliver. Nothing will change that. But Lady Bevan *is* your real mother. And she loves you more than anything in this world."

Oliver gazed at the woman whom he thought was his mother. "Will you still live at Heavensford?"

Josie, teary eyed, glanced at Lord and Lady Bevan. Simon acknowledged her with a smile. Her eyes shifted back to Oliver. "You are a brave beautiful boy. I will stay for a little while, but then I will have to go."

Oliver wrapped his arms around Josie's neck. "No! I don't want you to go."

"You will always have a place here at Heavensford, Josie. Not as a maid, but as the dear friend you have become." Alessandra reached out, grasped Josie's hand, and gave it a squeeze. "A dear, dear friend."

"You are my dear friend as well. But it is time for me to complete my own journey."

Simon watched the two women hug, Oliver wedged between them.

A tapping on the study door broke their embrace.

Sebastian entered, looked down at Simon, who raised a brow, then looked at the ladies, who were wiping their eyes, then looked at Oliver, who was clinging to the maid.

"Come join us, Sebastian," Alessandra motioned for her brother to sit next to her. "There is someone I want you to meet."

Chapter Fifty-Six

Sebastian examined the unrolled parchment, then looked at the three people before him, who were looking at him in anticipation of his response. He dropped the document onto the desk and went to where his sister was standing.

"Alessandra, why did you not tell me about Oliver?" The earl rubbed a hand through his hair. "He is an heir. To the Ashleigh estate! And you're his mother!"

"Do not upset your sister, Sebastian." Simon walked without falter, his voice unwavering. "It is a delicate situation."

"I am sure, but to not tell me? I just don't understand. You could have told me. Why was I not sent word that you were even with child?"

"Sebastian, there is much you will never know about my marriage to Cecil. Things...cruel things I do not want you to know. It is bad enough you have seen drawings of some of the treatment I received. I do not want to burden your thoughts more than they already are. As for Oliver, I was protecting him. And I had to keep on doing so."

"But how could I not be told of an impending addition to the family? And once you arrived in England, surely you could have revealed all this to me. I know I wronged you by letting our father take you away to America in the first place, but did my action, or lack thereof, warrant you to forbid me knowledge of your secret?"

"What would you have done had you been me, Sebastian? I could not let Cecil ruin another life. And I did not want Oliver growing up knowing that his father was a most horrid and cruel man who beat his mother at his every whim. It was bad enough that there had been times when the child had seen it happen. The yelling, the crying, the torture.

"As for not sending word, a missive was written at first knowledge of an impending blessing. But Cecil had control of all posts coming in...and going out." The marchioness glanced at Josie. Then Simon. Then back to her brother. "I contemplated what I was going to reveal to you during the journey home. But once I arrived and saw your expression..." Alessandra looked down at her debility. "The look of repulsion when you saw my...transformation. I had to continue hiding the true identity of Oliver. How could I not? I did not want you to look at him with disdain for what his father had done."

Sebastian knelt before his sister, taking hold of her hands. "I would not have done that to him, Alessandra. He is only a child. And not responsible for who his father was. Or what his father did."

"You say that with sincerity. But the risk was too high. And your sudden love of partaking alcohol increased that risk."

"I am sorry, dearest. Please believe me. It was my guilt at what happened to you that lead me to drink my days away."

"Cecil drank. And he was in quite a stupor the day Oliver was born. He was violent when sober, but there is no word to describe him when he was in his cups. If I would not have made him angry, he would not have chased me. And then I wouldn't have fallen. The pain was immediate. That was the first and only time Cecil looked worried. I had another month to go. I was too early."

"What happened next?" the earl asked as he led his sister to take a seat.

"Cecil left after the midwife arrived. When Oliver came into this world, he made not one sound. It was feared that he was stillborn, but then he took a breath. And then another. And yet another. Regardless, his entry into the world of the living was a quiet one. There was little time to react to the opportunity that presented itself. In order for Oliver to have a chance at a normal life, at a safe life, I had to give up my right to be his mother. I had to do the unthinkable, and give away the most gracious gift God could have ever given me."

"That is the black mark you alluded to on more than one occasion, is it not, sweet one?"

Alessandra answered Simon's question with a dip of her head, then continued to speak. "Oliver was placed in the midwife's basket and covered with one of the bloody sheets from my bed. I didn't have time to count his fingers or toes. It would have been too dangerous if I held him. Cecil was never the wiser that Oliver was alive."

"But Oliver *did* live with you, did he not?" her brother queried.

"The midwife took Oliver to her home, where her own daughter would become his wet nurse and raise him. The wet nurse was Josie."

"How did Josie and Oliver come to reside in your home?"

Alessandra pulled her hands from Sebastian's. She looked around the room, searching for Simon. He had become her rock, her strength. She watched as he tilted his head forward, encouraging her to continue, and silently acknowledged that he would come to her side if she needed him.

"The midwife had become extremely ill and died. Even though she learned to be a midwife from her mother, Josie had nowhere to go and no income. She couldn't leave Oliver at home alone had she been able to find employment. So she did the only thing she thought possible. Fearing living on the streets more than living with a deranged employer, Josie came to my house and begged Cecil for a job as my maid. At first he told her she needed to leave Oliver somewhere else, but when she was walking out the door with Oliver, he changed his mind. He said it would give him great pleasure to see me traumatized emotionally. That it would be further punishment for me to have another woman's child reside in my house, knowing that mine did not live past birth."

"So Cecil never knew then that Oliver was his?"

"No. Shortly after Josie came to be my maid, Cecil began to drink more heavily and host gambling parties almost every evening. The abuse became worse, if you can believe that. Especially when he lost at cards. And he lost more times than he won.

"The night he died, he had been accused of accosting a young girl. The girl's father was the owner of one of the taverns Cecil frequented. Edwin was with Cecil when the incident took place. Though the girl was beaten badly, she was not only able to give a brief testimony as to what transpired during the attack, but who the attackers were. My husband and his cohort never made it home that night. Their bodies were found the next morning. No one came forward as a witness to my husband's passing. Nor Edwin's. Therefore, no charges could be brought forth. Cecil and Edwin wreaked havoc on every establishment they would haunt. Finally, someone was not afraid to take action against them."

Alessandra looked about the room once more, then returned her attention to the earl.

Sebastian blinked away a tear. "My solicitor said your signature is on the entitlement transfer for the shipyard. Was Tucker Morris the girl's father?"

"Yes. As soon as I found out what happened, I went to see Mister Morris to apologize for what Cecil and Edwin had done. As retribution for what his daughter fell victim to, I signed over the shipyard to him. He has three other daughters, you see, besides the one who was attacked. I knew it was the right thing to do. I did not think you would find fault with my decision, Sebastian."

"No. I support it most strongly, dearest. It was a new business venture, one that our father thought was necessary, but it really was not needed. We have more than enough investments and properties here in England to keep our family line well supported. I will send Mister Meade a letter of agreement regarding the transfer."

"I'm glad you approve of my decision." Alessandra vacated her seat. "I am suddenly very tired from this discussion. I'm going to rest upstairs for a short spell or I will not be able to be a proper hostess to the rest of our guests. Please excuse me."

"I'll walk with you, my love." Simon kissed her hand before placing it in the crook of his arm. "You are quite the woman, sweet one."

Both remained silent until their chambers were reached. Alessandra put up a hand, stopping Simon from entering. "No, please go keep my brother company. You two have much to talk about, do you not?"

"I suppose you're right. You're sure you are fine then, my love?"

"With you in my life, I am much more than fine."

Alessandra stood on tiptoe and kissed her husband's cheek. She closed the door then, but knew sleep would evade her, even in a state of exhaustion.

She sat at her writing desk, opened her journal, dipped the quill into the bottle of black ink, and quietly began to write.

Dearest Journal,

Guilt is not easy to overcome. I am worried more for my brother, than I am for myself.

And what about Oliver? Would he ever accept me as his real mother? He loves me, that much I know, but only time will tell how this next chapter of my life, *our* lives, will unfold.

One thing I am certain of is that I love them both with my entire being. In essence, I have become a warrior and protector in my own right, have I not? For the son I tried to save from the hands of an evil doer, and for the brother who thinks himself responsible for the torture that had befallen me.

There is another I love just as much, dear journal, and that is my husband, who accepted my broken spirit and physically scarred shell of a body as though I were untouched.

I love him more than I thought I would be able to love again. He did as he vowed so often he would do. He saved me. Simon Thane Bevan, Marquess of Heavensford, warrior and protector of all who reside within it, has given me the strength to live.

And for that, my heart will only beat for him. Forever and always.

Epilogue

Bevan House, Mayfair, London, 1820

"Hush, girls," Oliver raised a finger to his lips. His sisters, Penelope, four, and Hermione, three, ignored his command. His third request in as many minutes for the girls to be silent only made the younger siblings giggle more. "Be quiet now. Stop giggling. Understand?"

"Okay, Ollie." Both sisters answered in unison. And of course, as most little girls do, they giggled. Uncontrollably.

Oliver rolled his eyes. "Why couldn't you both have been born brothers?" He crouched down to their eye level and spoke sternly. "Now hush I say. You're going to give us away."

Both girls, while born of the same parents, were not children born to Alessandra and Simon. Shortly after the marquess gave his family surname of Bevan to Oliver, the marchioness had found herself with child. Sadly, carrying the babe did not last past the fourth month. And so it was, three times more.

The physician attending Alessandra blamed it on the beatings the marchioness had suffered throughout her first marriage; stating that her body was left too weak to sustain the strength needed when enceinte. It was found, in the physician's opinion, that further anticipation of expecting any child born of the marchioness be dismissed.

Following the sorrowful news, the marquess took his wife and Oliver for a brief stay in Wales. It was here that the marquess' cousin, the Duke of Veston, Quinlan Michael Blackburn, introduced the couple to the children of the local orphanage. The children, the duke told Alessandra, were not only found living on the streets in the poorest areas of London and elsewhere, but some had been rescued from abusive homes by the Duke of Veston himself. Two such children were sisters Penelope and Hermione.

Their father was an iniquitous pickpocket, who used his young daughters as a distraction during his sticky-finger escapades. His plan worked to his advantage...most of the time. But when it didn't...

Penelope's limp was one of those times. As was Hermione's facial scar, which started at the outer corner of her eye and ended at the corner of her mouth. Alessandra also learned that the girls gained no sanctuary in their alcoholic mother.

Upon hearing of their plight, the Duke of Veston was given permission to take the children...for a price. The girls' father was only too happy to be rid of them for a fee of one hundred pounds; to which he signed an oath that he, nor his wife, would ever seek the girls' whereabouts, or try to reclaim their rights as their parents. The mother, so engulfed in her cups, was barely cognizant when she signed her name to the agreement.

After their formal introduction, Penelope and Hermione spent the next few days at the duke's estate. It became quite clear, and in immediate fashion, that the girls, though not their own biologically, most assuredly belonged to the marquess and his wife.

Alessandra, whose faith was stronger than it had been in previous years, recognized this as God's plan for her all along. That her own dreadful plight was preparation for what was needed of her. And that was to save these young girls.

The marchioness did not hesitate. Guardianship of the siblings was sought and granted without delay. They were now part of the Bevan family.

Oliver tried to quiet his new sisters once more, but voices outside the library door did what Oliver's could not. The children looked at each other from their hiding spots; Oliver behind the marquess' leather wingback chair, and the two girls behind a smaller version, fashioned in light blue upholstery belonging to the marchioness.

Hermione mimicked her brother's action from a moment before, and put her tiny pointer finger up to her lips.

The door opened. "I wonder where the children have gone. No sooner did Nanny leave for her afternoon off and the trio disappeared."

"My guess would be that the girls are playing dress up in the attic, and Oliver is the handsome prince sent to dance with them at their ball."

"Penelope likes bugs, dear husband. I do not see her wanting to play dress up."

"That is true. Perhaps she is a mighty queen guarding her younger sister from a fiery dragon."

"Oooh, I like that better than your games, Ollie." Penelope quickly put a hand up to cover her mouth.

"Hush, Penelope!"

Simon winked at his wife. "Did you hear something, my love?"

"What do you think that was? I hope it wasn't the puppy. I wanted so dearly to surprise Oliver."

"And don't forget the kittens for the girls."

"I wonder if that noise was one of the kittens then."

Simon and Alessandra fought back their own giggles.

"Oliver has become quite the young man, sweet one."

"I'm proud of him, Simon. He's protective of his sisters

and allows them to follow him wherever he goes."

"And he's given up frogs from what I hear. Oakes told me himself that he hasn't seen a frog in weeks."

"I'm so glad. I have not been blessed with finding any in my own belongings and I hope it stays that way."

Simon motioned for Alessandra to look at her embroidery basket, sitting on the floor next to her chair. There was a slight movement coming from inside.

She turned back towards Simon, who arched a brow.

"But if I do happen to find a frog in my things, I would give it to Cook. I hear the French claim eating frog legs to be a delicious delicacy."

Penelope and Hermione scrunched their faces. Oliver's eyes widened. All three remained silent behind the chairs.

"You know, my love, should it come to pass that Oliver did hide a frog in your belongings, the puppy will need to be given away."

"You did tell him that frogs were banned from inside the house. And since the girls are nowhere to be found either, then their kittens will have to go."

"It is only fair, sweet one. If all three are guilty, then all three will forfeit their surprises."

"No, I want my kitten!" Penelope grabbed Hermione's hand and pulled her from behind the chair. "We want our kittens, do we not, Hermione?"

"It was Ollie," stated the younger of the two sisters.

"Aw, girls...who needs them?" Oliver slowly brought himself into view.

"Oliver." Simon faced the children, arms akimbo. "Did you and your sisters hide a frog in your mother's embroidery basket?"

"It was Ollie, papa."

"Yes, I heard you the first time, Hermione. But now I am talking to your brother." The corner of Simon's mouth tilted upward.

"It was all in fun, Father. I swear."

"Bevans do not swear, lad. We promise."

Oliver looked at the marchioness, who was having difficulty suppressing a smile. "I'm sorry, Mother. It was all in fun. I promise. It won't happen again."

"Are you really going to give the frog to Cook?"

"That depends, Penelope. Do you want to eat frog legs for dinner?"

"No! Neither does Hermione. Do you, Hermione?"

Hermione scrunched her face while shaking her head, dark curls swung back and forth. "It was Ollie."

That did it. Alessandra let loose the laugh she was holding back since entering the room.

Simon, trying with little success to hinder his own joviality, asked Oliver the same question.

"No, Father. I don't want to eat the frog's legs. He's a harmless creature. Truly he is. It's not his fault I hid him in Mother's basket."

"Then I suggest you put him back outside where he belongs. And no more bringing those things in this house."

"I promise, Father."

When Oliver returned from releasing the frog back into the outdoors, the family followed Simon into the sitting room. There, in a corner, were three small wooden crates. Barely audible meows and whining could be heard from the topless packages. The children ran to retrieve their surprises.

"Oh, isn't she lovely?" Penelope picked up her solid gray with white paws kitten.

"Look at mine, Pen!" Hermione pointed to hers, gray with black stripes, and white paws.

"She's beautiful, Hermione."

Penelope laid her kitten next to Hermione's. "There. Now they won't be alone. They will always have each other."

Once the girls were satisfied that their kittens were comfortable, they turned towards their brother, who was sitting on the floor crossed legged, the puppy in his lap.

"Can we pet him, Ollie?"

"Yes, but be careful. He doesn't like to be around girls." The brown and white, with a touch of black, Rough Collie lay quietly as he licked his new master's fingers.

"How do you know he doesn't like girls? You just got him, Ollie."

"I just know. And don't you be putting ribbons and bonnets on him. He's a boy."

"We won't Ollie, will we Hermione?"

"No."

"What are you going to name your puppy, Ollie?"

"I don't know. Why don't we all sit in a circle and try to come up with names?"

"Okay. Come on Hermione. Get your kitten."

Once the children formed their circle, they placed their pets in the center. Alessandra and Simon sat amongst the children, happy to have been included in the quest of selecting names for the latest additions to the family.

"What about...eww...what is that smell?" Penelope pinched the end of her nose.

Hermione did the same.

Alessandra followed suit. As did Simon, who waved a hand in front of his face. He tried in vain to remove the stink from his proximity. "Good grief, I think the puppy has some gas issues."

Oliver remained unaffected by the odor.

"Ollie, your dog smells."

"He does not, Penelope."

"He does too, and you know he does. Didn't his dog fart and now he smells, Hermione?"

The youngest of the family looked around at the members of the circle before giving her response with a giggle. "It was Ollie."

ABOUT THE AUTHOR

Saving Alessandra is Christine Maria Jahn's debut novel. She studied English Literature in college and has a passion for historical fiction. She is the mother of three and lives in Virginia, where she is currently working on her second novel.

Made in the USA
Charleston, SC
12 February 2016